Will to Win

Samantha Alexander lives in Lincolnshire with a variety of animals including her thoroughbred horse, Bunny, and a pet goose called Bertie. Her schedule is almost as busy and exciting as her plots – she writes a number of columns for newspapers and magazines, is a teenage agony aunt for BBC Radio Leeds and in her spare time she regularly competes in dressage and showjumping.

D0716963

Also by Samantha Alexander
and available from Macmillan

RIDERS

2 Team Spirit   December 1996
3 Peak Performance   January 1997
4 Rising Star   February 1997

HOLLYWELL STABLES

1 Flying Start
2 The Gamble
3 Revenge
4 Fame
5 The Mission
6 Trapped
7 Running Wild
8 Secrets

RIDERS

1

Will to Win

SAMANTHA ALEXANDER

MACMILLAN CHILDREN'S BOOKS

First published 1996 by
Macmillan Children's Books
a division of Macmillan Publishers Limited
25 Eccleston Place, London SW1W 9NF
and Basingstoke

Associated companies throughout the world

ISBN 0 330 34533 8

1 3 5 7 9 8 6 4 2

A CIP catalogue record for this book is available from the British Library.

Printed by Mackays of Chatham PLC, Chatham, Kent.

To my parents for their constant support and encouragement and for putting up with me when writer's block strikes.

Samantha Alexander and Macmillan Children's Books would like to thank *Horse and Pony* magazine for helping us by running a competition to find our cover girl, Sally Johnson. Look out for more about the **Riders** and **Hollywell Stables** series in *Horse and Pony* magazine and find out more about Samantha by reading her agony column in every issue.

Macmillan Children's Books would also like to thank Chris White; and David Burrows and all at Sandridgebury Stables, especially Toby and his owner Sylvie.

And finally thanks to Angela Clarke from Ride-Away in Sutton-on-Forest, Yorkshire for providing the riding clothes, hats and boots featured on the covers.

CHARACTERS

Alexandra Johnson Our heroine. 14 years old. Blonde, brown eyes. Ambitious, strong-willed and determined to become a top eventer. Owns Barney, a 14.2 hh dun with black points.

Ash Burgess Our hero. 19 years old. Blond hair, blue eyes, flashy smile. Very promising young eventer. He runs the livery stables for his parents. His star horse is Donavon, a 16.2 hh chestnut.

Zoe Jackson Alex's best friend. 14 years old. Sandy hair, freckles. Owns Lace, a 14.1 hh grey.

Camilla Davies Typical Pony Club high-flyer. 15 years old. Owns The Hawk, a 14.2 hh bay.

Judy Richards Ash's head groom and sometime girlfriend. 18 years old.

Eric Burgess Ash's uncle. Around 50 years old. His legs were paralysed in a riding accident. He has a basset hound called Daisy.

Look out for the definition-packed glossary of horsey terms at the back of the book.

CHAPTER ONE

"But don't you see?" I spun round. "It's my big chance, my only chance. I've got to prove everybody wrong!"

Zoe looked at me with a blank expression and proceeded to rip open a packet of crisps. "Alex Johnson, I'll never understand you. You own a horse with a reputation for being a complete maniac and you think you can waltz into your first competition and win."

"I don't think," I threw back at her. "I know."

I'd wanted to be a top rider since the very first time I'd seen a horse pass by the front gate of our house. Then I saw Badminton Horse Trials on television and my future was mapped out. I was going to be a champion Event rider – the best in the world – and nothing was going to stop me. My parents didn't know anything about horses but gave in and bought Barney for me. He wasn't expensive because of his reputation for being difficult after he was involved in a road accident.

"I don't think the careers officer was very convinced." Zoe read my thoughts.

At fourteen years old we were being grilled at school about future career prospects and exam options. Mrs Maplin, our careers officer, had been convinced I'd make a first grade secretary and was still reeling from the shock of me storming out of her classroom.

"Alex, why do you have to be so intense?" Zoe screwed up the crisp bag and gave me one of her quirky looks.

We'd been best friends for three months, ever since my parents had moved to the area and I'd started at the local school. Now I had my pony at the same stable yard as Zoe, the Burgess yard, which was the best in the county. My horse Barney was 14.2 hands high, but had more oomph than most seventeen-hand horses. He was dun with black points.

"Of course," Zoe carried on regardless, "you could always ask Ash to give you some lessons."

Ash Burgess, nicknamed Flash in the event world because he was so fast and glamorous when riding cross-country, was already being hailed as the next Mark Todd. He ran his business (livery, training and competing) from the stables his parents owned and had recently left college to compete full time. His horses were fantastic and made me drool with envy. Zoe said girls usually drooled over Ash, not his horses. He was gorgeous but he had a definite attitude problem. At the moment he was away competing in Ireland. I had to admit, I was dying to meet him.

"Oh no!" Zoe had just stood up to stretch her legs. She wheeled round in the doorway and I could immediately tell that something was wrong.

"It's Barney," she yelled. "He's gone!"

"What?" I ran out of the feed room. I couldn't believe it. The stable door swung open, empty, the bolt pulled back. I was so sure I'd put his special clip on. "Barney!"

"He's heading straight for the main gate!" Ash's head groom, Judy, clattered into the yard leading two horses and looking sweaty and hot. "I've warned you, Alex, you've got to get him under control."

But I was already running, streaking down the tarmac drive, arms and legs flailing all over the place. If only I'd been wearing trainers instead of rubber riding boots. "Barney, where are you?"

He'd done this before, opened the stable door with his teeth, but he'd never actually left the yard. If he got on to the main road, into the traffic, heaven knows what would happen. Barney was terrified of lorries. He'd had a terrible accident a couple of years ago when he'd bolted down a motorway: the rider broke her hip and Barney nearly died. "Please God, let him be all right."

My lungs were hurting, I could hardly get my breath. The Burgess drive was over half a mile long, cutting through dense parkland, and I wasn't anywhere near the end. If the gate was open . . . If anything happened to Barney . . .

"Hey you!" The roar of a motorbike engine cut through my panic and nearly sent me sprawling head over heels. The last thing I expected to see was a bright red four-wheeler bike powering

3

through the trees towards me with some idiot on top of it driving at God knows how many miles an hour.

He raced across, shouting and waving towards a field on the edge of the parkland. "Well don't just stand there," he yelled. "Go and catch him!"

It was then that I spotted Barney. He was galloping in circles, his legs scuffing up a cloud of soil, his head and neck stuck out in the wind, oblivious to anything but his pounding hoofs.

"He's going like the clappers." The guy flipped up the visor of his crash helmet to reveal striking blue eyes. "That field's only just been set – he's ripping it to pieces!"

"Well if you hadn't set him off with that stupid bike in the first place!"

"Don't shout at me."

"I'll shout all I like," I yelled back. "That's my pony going crazy down there and it's all your fault!"

"Have you any idea who I am?"

"I couldn't care less if you were the Emperor of China, now get out of my way!"

Barney eventually pulled up, covered in frothy sweat, snorting like an express train. His head collar was hanging round his neck and there were lumps of soil stuck to his mane. He was heaving for breath and I was scared stiff he was going to keel over with a heart attack.

"Look what you've done," I screeched. "You've nearly killed him!"

"What I've done?" The guy looked incredulous. "A whole field's just been ruined by that scraggy nag."

I was livid. The last thing I needed was a buffoon like him giving me a sermon. I was worried about Barney. His tendons felt as if they were burning up.

"You needn't get hysterical," he said. "He's perfectly all right, it might even have knocked some sense into him."

"Oh you, you . . ." I was so hopping mad I couldn't get any words out.

Suddenly he broke into a grin, and gave me another flash of his dazzling eyes. He was about nineteen with blond hair and strong tanned arms.

I pretended not to notice him watching as I undid the lead rope tied round my waist.

"Here, take my jacket. You're trembling."

"No thank you," I bit back. "I'm perfectly OK, and besides, I wouldn't know where to return it."

I quickly knotted the lead rope into a make-shift rein and, still shaking, vaulted on to Barney's back. He was really sticky and I had to grip with my knees to stop myself slipping off.

"No doubt I'll be seeing you again," he smiled up at me, showing perfect white teeth.

I felt my stomach curl into a tight ball.

"Not if I can help it," I snapped back, jerking

my chin in the air and wheeling Barney round on his hocks. "Oh and by the way," I looked over my shoulder, a mouthful of hair whipping into my face, "find something out about horses before you start lecturing other people."

I trotted off with the uncomfortable feeling that his eyes were boring straight into my back.

"You did what?" Zoe was even more gobsmacked than I imagined. "You said that? And what did he say?" Her amber eyes were flashing like traffic lights.

It had taken ages to rub Barney down and he was now safely in his stable with no water until he had properly cooled off. I found Zoe in the tack room drooling over a picture of a pure bred Arab in the pony magazine, *In The Saddle*. She soon put it down when I told her my story.

"But Alex . . ."

"And I told him to find out something about horses before lecturing people."

"Oh Alex . . ."

"He won't be so cocky next time, I can promise you."

"But Alex" – she sounded desperate – "you don't understand!"

The red four-wheel bike pulled up in front of the main stable block just as I was about to repeat the whole conversation.

Judy ran out in obvious excitement, smoothing her hair down, her lips splashed with lipstick.

At exactly the same moment a huge white aluminium horsebox with a red flash down either side manoeuvred into the yard. The guy on the bike took off his crash helmet to reveal stunning ash blond hair, and affectionately kissed Judy on the cheek.

"You've really done it this time," Zoe squeaked, turning beetroot and tugging at one of her sandy curls. "You know who that is, don't you? That's Ash Burgess!"

CHAPTER TWO

"You can't avoid him for ever." Zoe caught me up on Lace, her pretty grey mare, who never seemed to put a foot wrong.

"I'm not," I insisted, readjusting the chin strap on my jockey skull and shoving back long strands of blonde hair. I kept threatening to have it all cut off like Zoe's but everybody said I wouldn't look half so wild.

"I'm not avoiding him," I repeated. "Just making sure our paths don't cross."

I'd been skulking around all morning, diving behind stable doors if I happened to spot Ash. It was a nightmare. Then I noticed Barney had chewed a huge hole in his door frame overnight and I had to ram it full of newspaper and straw. Ash nearly caught me in the act and I had to bribe a kid with a Shetland pony to distract him while I bolted back to the tack room and begged Zoe's parents to fetch me some woodfiller. Zoe's mum, Patsy, was convinced I was slightly demented and spent half an hour debating and twiddling with her head scarf before reluctantly setting off for the hardware store.

We hadn't got out on a ride till lunchtime and now there was a faint drizzle of rain.

"He's getting worse." Zoe stated the obvious and I felt like throttling her. For the last hour Barney had been dancing sideways, tugging at my arms, snatching at the reins with the strength of a bulldozer.

It was the first time I'd tried him in a pelham bit, but it might as well have been a roll of cotton wool for all the good it was doing.

"Admit it, Alex, he's hopeless. There's no way you'll ever be able to take him cross-country."

I immediately felt my cheeks burn and the blood start pounding in my head. I'd suffered heaven knows how many jokes about Barney needing new brakes and booking him into the local garage. It wasn't his fault that he'd been mistreated or that his mouth had gone hard.

"All right, Miss Clever Clogs, I'll prove it to you." I was angry now, furious. Nobody criticized Barney, nobody. I'd had just about all I could take. "You see that tyre jump over there." I pointed. "I bet Barney can jump it as well as Lace *and* pull up at the other side."

"Alex . . . don't be such a fool. You'll kill your—"

But I'd already set off.

"Steady, Barney, steady." I steeled my body in the saddle, gripping with my knees and pushing my heels well down in the stirrups. "Now come on, Barney, we can't mess up. You've got to behave. Let's show Zoe once and for all."

The tyre jump was only about two foot nine

but it looked spooky and there was a clump of nettles at the front. We'd never jumped tyres before. Even worse, the approach was slightly downhill.

"Steady, boy, steady." He was plunging and leaping all over the place.

I turned in a wide arc so we had a good line to the fence and enough time to get organized.

"Alex, don't do it!" Zoe cantered across on Lace waving frantically from the other side of the jump.

"Come on, boy, come on." I leant further forward and felt Barney's mane lift up in the wind, felt his stride lengthen. It was brilliant, it was like riding at Becher's Brook.

One, two, three. Barney cocked one ear forward and one back and launched into the air two strides too early. He soared over the tyres as if they were nothing and within seconds we were back on solid ground, Barney grasping the bit and dragging me forward.

And that's when it all went wrong.

I just didn't regain my balance fast enough.

"Alex!" Zoe and Lace had become a blur.

Barney accelerated into a flat-out gallop with his head stuck down and me out of control. I heaved on the reins but there was no reaction. He didn't even know I was there. It was as if he'd changed into another horse.

Panic crept into my throat and made me want to scream out. I had to stay calm. My bare hands were already hurting from the constant pulling, my eyes stinging from the wind and rain.

"Barney, stop, please." I yanked first on one rein and then on the other, jabbing him as hard as I could, doing everything you're not supposed to do.

We reached the edge of the wood and Barney made straight for a log suspended off the ground into a three-foot cross-country jump. I knew all the jumps in the parkland. I'd drawn diagrams and studied them at home under the bedcovers late at night. And I knew we were going much too fast. He'd clip the top for sure or miss the take-off altogether.

I leaned back and pulled but his head just went down further and the jump rushed towards us. I shortened my reins, sat still in the saddle and tried to look directly into the middle of the fence just like all the famous eventers. I tried to ignore the cold fear in the pit of my stomach, the knot of anxiety in my chest. "Please, Barney, please, slow down!"

We took off a stride out.

I got left behind but was quick enough to let the reins run through my fingers right to the buckle. Barney stretched for it and we were clear, me gripping in the saddle like a monkey, all hunched up.

There was a track zig-zagging through the wood which I hadn't explored before. A soft sandy track artificially made which meandered through the trees. Barney was like a cat, twisting this way and that, still pounding forward, his sides heaving.

I gathered up the reins and tried to catch my left stirrup. It was all happening so fast. I knew I had to hold on.

The post and rail fence on the other side of the wood was big, solid and the type Ash Burgess would pop over as a warm-up. It wasn't meant for 14.2-hand ponies out of control.

There was nothing I could do. I just sat as quietly as possible, so as not to interfere with his balance. I'd read in countless books that the worst thing you can do when approaching a fence is to start flapping your arms and legs. It only upset the horse. I was already picturing Barney hitting the top rail, somersaulting right over, landing on top of me, squashing me to death.

He met the jump just right.

It was fantastic. The perfect take-off. The power. The speed. The rush of adrenalin. He touched down and picked up again like a champion, bounding away in long effortless strides. I kept my eyes tightly shut, fear mingled with excitement. It was incredible.

But the moment didn't last long. It suddenly dawned on me that we were careering downhill, skimming across mole hills, still picking up speed. My legs were getting weaker. The saddle was starting to slip, disappearing underneath me.

"Barney, stop!" We charged straight down the hill, leapt over a stream and ploughed straight across someone's beautifully mown lawn, under some trees, into some runner beans and finally, I went flying unceremoniously into a flower bed. Barney skidded to a halt.

"Barney, how could you?" I looked up, spluttered out a mouthful of damp peat and surveyed the picture of devastation. A carpet of bright yellow flowers lay bashed and flattened, completely ruined.

Barney's saddle was under his stomach, his reins hanging down, his whole body slicked wet with sweat, and some kind of twig or bush trailing in his tail. Despite all this, he gleefully took off down a path, nudged the lid off a rainwater butt and plunged in his oversized head.

"Barney!" I leapt up, peat-blackened and exhausted but determined to stop him.

"What the hell do you think you're doing?" The voice terrified me. I hadn't realized that we were being watched. I hardly dared turn round.

"You stupid, stupid girl."

I noticed the wheelchair first. Then the strong sinewy arms, the knotty hands, the lined face hardened with temper. "Look at my lawn, look what you've done to my flowers!"

He was going crazy. I took two steps backwards and crashed into a garden seat. Barney looked up, vegetation streaming from his mouth and then started pawing at the cabbages, getting ready to roll.

"Well don't just stand there, stop him!"

The old man was going berserk. I thought he was going to have a heart attack. He kept pounding the armrests with his fists, shaking with rage. If he'd had something to throw at me I think he would have done.

"Get that saddle off him quick! Don't stand about looking foolish!"

I grabbed hold of the broken reins and gently eased Barney out of the cabbages, tempting him with a sugar lump I'd found in my pocket. His eyes rolled wickedly and I knew he was planning something.

"Bring him over here, stand him on the level ground, look sharp!"

Barney took one look at the wheelchair and froze in horror. I don't think he was really frightened, it was just a great excuse to play up. And that meant rearing.

"Get down!" The old man let out such a fierce growl that Barney came back on to all fours, trembling like a dog and not daring to move.

"Good boy, very good boy." The voice immediately changed to smooth, deep tones laced with praise. Barney didn't know whether he was coming or going. I think he'd finally met his match.

"How did you do that?"

The old man didn't answer. He was locked into his own world, shuffling round Barney in his wheelchair, looking at his teeth, his eyes, feeling all down his legs, manoeuvring round the back, lifting up his tail and staring at his hocks. Finally he pushed the wheels backwards and sat in a trance.

Barney stared back at him, the whites of his eyes not showing for once.

"So, so what's wrong with him?" I was genuinely nervous.

"Him? Oh no, the problem's not him. It's you! You're going to have to learn to ride!"

I was totally shocked. How dare he be so insulting? How dare he talk to me like that? Hot tears of anger prickled behind my eyes. I could feel my hands starting to shake.

"And it's no good going all girlie. That's not going to solve anything."

He shuffled forward and handed me a checked handkerchief. "That's not for your nose, it's to wipe all that soil off your chin."

"Oh."

He was so abrasive. He sat there, steely grey hair blowing up in the wind, watery blue eyes darting like quickfire. He was dressed in a crisp shirt and a tie, yet there were gardening gloves pushed down the side of his chair and dirt under his nails. Who was he? Why did no one know about this cottage? Why was he never seen?

"Alex?" Zoe trotted up on Lace who was snorting slightly and skittering sideways. "I've been looking everywhere."

The old man took one glance at her and started wheeling frantically back to the house.

"Learn to ride that horse!" he shouted over

16

his shoulder and then disappeared through some patio doors, drawing some curtains shut, blocking out all sign of life.

"Who was that man? And what's happened here?" Zoe stared around in amazement at the blitzed garden. "Blimey, Alex. It's a tip!"

I led Barney home because I was too shaken up to ride. He lolled along, his head slung low, dragging his hind legs.

"I don't understand it." I went through it all again, my mind racing.

"It seems pretty clear to me," Zoe said. "You wrecked his garden, he bawled you out. That's the second dressing down you've had in as many days."

"Yes, but you're missing the point." I peeled off my jockey skull, letting my hair stream out, rubbing at my forehead, half with itchiness, half with frustration.

"Don't you see?" I said, getting excited. "He didn't criticize Barney. For the first time someone actually saw his potential. Zoe, he believes in him!"

CHAPTER THREE

"It's in the common room. A white envelope. You can't miss it." Zoe leant over the stable door where I was grooming Barney. She didn't seem to know quite how to act.

The common room was an old building next to the feed room which was used by everybody to generally hang out. It was equipped with a kettle, a fridge, a pool table, a dart board, comfy chairs. It was great for rainy days, but up till now I'd stayed well away.

"It's addressed to you, Alex. Everybody's been looking at it all morning."

I was worried. A letter addressed to me could only mean one thing: we were being asked to leave. Judy had already suggested as much, and what if that old man had complained to Ash?

"It might not be that bad." Zoe twiddled with one of her curls, which suggested she thought it was. "Alex, calm down. You're panicking."

I quickly washed my hands in the automatic waterer, which Barney refused point blank to use, preferring his well worn black plastic bucket. He looked at me almost with reproach as I unclipped his lead rope. He was so used to an hour's intensive grooming a day he couldn't understand why I was breaking off after ten minutes. He stared down at his feet as if to tell me he needed some hoof oil.

"If that pony gets any more human he'll be sleeping with a teddy bear." Zoe took a compact out of her pocket and quickly applied some lip gloss. She'd just discovered make-up and was driving me mad with the choice between shell pink and tangerine orange. "Did you know," she carefully pressed her lips together, "that toothpaste takes away love bites?"

I marched across the gravel yard trying to keep my cool. A couple of ducks called Nigel and Reggie waddled off in a huff because I didn't have any bread. They spent all day wandering around trying to get into the stables to pinch the corn.

The arrangement my parents had at the Burgess yard was different from that of the other owners. We rented the stable and I looked after Barney myself. And I had to help out at weekends: cleaning tack, raking the outdoor manege, scrubbing out mangers – all the usual chores. All the other horses got full livery so their riders could just turn up and ride.

It would be quite easy for them to ask me to leave. Maybe they'd found another owner who could afford to pay full price?

My palms were sweating as I walked along the wooden veranda, past a glamorous bright chestnut gelding and a rose grey mare who both belonged to Ash Burgess, and into the common room.

Luckily the only person there was Jenny, a slightly dotty widow in her fifties whose horse, Gypsy Fair, was everything she lived for. She spent hours making up delicious, nutritious feeds with grated carrot, treacle, molasses and special herbal concoctions. Gypsy had turned into a hypochondriac knowing that she just had to stretch the wrong way and Jenny would give her a week off work.

The envelope was there, propped up on the fridge with a box of tea bags.

My heart did a somersault. It was a starchy white envelope with "For Alex" on it in spidery writing. It looked as if it had been written with a fountain pen. In the top right corner was written "Private".

My hands started shaking. Jenny clattered around noisily and then disappeared with a bucket and a packet of Epsom salts. I was alone. I quickly ripped the envelope open and stared down at the sharp writing. It was disjointed and barely legible. But it wasn't what I expected.

It rambled on about Barney and putting him in a snaffle and lowering the bit a couple of holes because it was too high in his mouth. Then something about trying a Grackle noseband.

It was signed "Eric" and then there was a PS: "We met yesterday and what are you going to do about my lawn?"

I must have read it six times. A snaffle – what was he on about? I'd never be able to hold Barney in a snaffle. And what was a Grackle? My mind was racing. I'd better ride over there this morning . . .

"So it *is* you?" The voice in the doorway made me freeze with horror. He'd got me cornered. There was no escape. It was Ash Burgess.

"I thought I recognized you yesterday when you dived behind the feed bins. You really ought to be more sociable. And that woolly hat really didn't suit you."

I felt my face colouring up. He was grinning at me, but half teasing, half condescending. "I think you've got something to tell me, don't you?"

"Who's Eric?" I blurted the words out before I had a chance to think.

It hit him like a sledgehammer. He almost rocked back on his heels. The teasing blue eyes suddenly turned steely hard and his soft curving mouth, which Zoe was always going on about, pulled back in a narrow line. I'd really done it now: talk about putting a match to a bonfire, it looked as if I'd set off World War Three.

"How the hell do you know about him?"

I backed up two steps, the letter scrunched up in my hand. "There's no need to fly off the handle." My voice jittered with nerves. He was glaring at me like a maniac.

"Just stay away from him, do you hear?" His hand gripped the door frame until the knuckles turned white. "Keep out of it, just mind your own business."

"And what if I don't?" The words escaped before I could stop them.

"Then you'll be looking for another stable."

"Be careful, Alex, that's all I can say." Zoe's face had filled with apprehension when I showed her the letter and explained about Ash. "He's no pushover, he generally means what he says."

I tightened Barney's girth a couple of holes and fiddled with the cross-over noseband which Judy had found in the tack room. Apparently a Grackle noseband helps to stop a horse opening its mouth and fighting the bit. It was murder to put on and Barney was already scowling like a baby. He ground his teeth together and threw me a disgusted look.

Zoe pushed Lace into a walk and started warming up in rising trot. For the first time in ages we had the manege to ourselves. Usually Judy or Ash were practising dressage or one of the livery owners got there first. The soft sand scuffed up in a lazy cloud as Zoe applied more leg and tried to get Lace to track up.

I swung into the saddle and felt Barney tense with temper. There were huge mirrors down either side of the arena and I could see him stomping along.

"Anyone would think he'd got clogs on," Zoe giggled.

But the only thing on my mind was Ash Burgess.

He and Judy had taken three horses in the lorry to practise steeplechasing over at a racehorse trainer's. The bright chestnut I'd been admiring for days was, according to Zoe, called Donavon and a likely bet for Badminton next year. He'd already won the Young Riders' National Championships and Ash was very protective of him. He looked incredible as he swung out of his stable in a brilliant white rug with a red flash and Ash's initials in the corner.

Ash clambered into the driver's seat wearing a leather jacket and white jods and never gave me a second glance. What he didn't know was that earlier in the afternoon I'd sneaked through the groom's door and sat revelling in the living quarters, looking at all the tack, the fridge, bunk beds, mini-cooker, dreaming about life as a famous eventer.

But there were no clues, nothing to suggest who Eric was or how he was linked to Ash. Nothing to say why he hid away in a cottage on the estate and why nobody knew of his existence. It was weird. And what's more, it was niggling away at me like an itchy rash. Just what was the big dark secret?

"Alex, it's working!" Zoe pulled up Lace and nodded towards Barney.

I'd been vaguely trotting a figure of eight with my thoughts totally on Ash and hadn't noticed Barney slowly giving in to the Grackle. When I looked down his neck was flexed, his nose tucked in and his mouth firmly closed. For once I wasn't being yanked all over the place.

"It's a miracle," Zoe squeaked. "He looks wonderful."

Normally Barney barged along with his neck stuck out like a giraffe. Now I tweaked on the reins and he came instantly back to a steady trot, still in a good shape.

"You know, he might even be able to do dressage, after all." Zoe patted Lace's grey coat, for the first time taking Barney seriously.

I was silently whooping for joy. I leapt off and showered Barney's nose with kisses. Then I hugged his neck. Then I pulled his ears. Zoe was already suggesting some jumping.

"I can't believe it," I gasped, my eyes filling with tears. "He really did look good, didn't he?"

Suddenly a dog appeared. That's if you could call it a dog – it had ears so long they were trailing on the ground and it was loping along like an extra large sausage dog.

"Who on earth does that belong to?" Zoe held firmly on to Lace, who was backing off with a look of anxiety.

Barney stood and stared in total bemusement. The dog, whose nose had been down to the ground like a hoover, suddenly looked up and let out a long friendly howl.

"It's a basset hound," Zoe said. "You know, as in Fred Basset."

"It's gorgeous," I drooled, watching it plop

down near one of the jumps and look across with big doleful eyes. "Maybe it's lost?"

Barney, who was equally fascinated, bounded forward, nearly treading on both my feet. "What the . . ." Before I could stop him he was shoving his nose into the dog's and making friends.

"It's a girl!" I shouted back to Zoe. "And she's got no collar! You poor poor sweetheart, where are you from, eh?" I knelt down, stroking her velvet soft ears and immediately falling in love. "Oh Zoe, she's beautiful."

"We can't keep her."

"I know, I know, but we can't leave her here either."

"So what are we going to do?"

Lace was rooted to the spot with her eyes on stalks while Barney was carrying on as if he'd just found a lifelong friend.

I rummaged in my pocket for a piece of chocolate. It was all sticky and covered in hay seeds but she wolfed it down in seconds. Then she plonked a huge brown and white paw on my foot which felt like a ton weight and gazed up at me with adoring eyes. "Oh Zoe, how could anybody not want her?"

The yard was deserted, not a soul in sight. There was nobody to ask for advice.

"We don't know she's been abandoned." Zoe hitched Lace's reins over her neck, ready to take her back to the stable. "All basset hounds look sad – it's part of their appeal."

"Here, take Barney." I purposefully dragged

him back to Zoe with his face set like thunder. "I'll take the dog into the feed room."

"You'll have to be quick!" Zoe dived out of the way as Barney cannoned into Lace's left shoulder. "Look, she's getting away!"

I couldn't believe how fast a basset hound could move. I wheeled round to see an elongated brown and white body bobbing across the manege, ears flying, tail stuck in the air and my brand new dressage whip trailing helplessly across the sand.

"I told you not to be sucked in," Zoe howled with laughter.

"But she's got my whip," I mumbled. "Zoe, she's running off with my best whip."

"Here doggy, doggy." I set off in pursuit, not having a clue where I was going. I'd last seen a glimpse of her disappearing in the direction of the main house. I'd never been this far out of the stable yard before and if anybody caught me they'd be convinced I was snooping.

"Come on girl, where are you?" I put both fingers in my mouth and whistled, but it didn't do any good. The only noise was a squirrel scampering up a beech tree. It was all very quiet.

The main house was solid grey stone, imposing, with an almost spooky quality. There was a sweeping gravel drive round the back and a huge conservatory with the door pinned open by a log. There were plants everywhere, great frondy things in porcelain tubs, and a cluttered array of wellington boots kicked into a corner.

The floor was black and white parquet with thick, black, muddy paw prints streaked across it. A dog's paw prints, a basset hound's most likely.

I stepped into a massive hallway the size of a barn and immediately felt small and insignificant. I'd taken off my riding boots and was plodding around in odd socks.

There were hunting prints everywhere, foxes' heads, a portrait of a big black horse looking over a stable door. A grandfather clock ticked noisily at the foot of the stairs and there, lying by a fancy table with an old-fashioned telephone, was my dressage whip.

"Hello?" I stood up thinking I'd heard footsteps. "Hello, anybody there?"

The photographs stared out at me as if insulted that I hadn't noticed them sooner. Beautiful framed shots of horses eventing, splashing through water, flying over solid Grand National type hedges. The whole wall under the stairs was chock-a-block: loads of Ash, one in top hat and tails, another leaping off a bank on what looked like Donavon, perfectly coordinated, looking for the next jump – a winning team.

My heart was thudding with excitement. There were a couple of pictures of riders receiving medals and someone standing next to them, smartly dressed in jacket and bowler hat, patting one of the horses. I didn't recognize Ash in any of them. Maybe it was his mother or a sister. The four medal winners were all women.

My eyes moved on to another picture, the same man in the bowler hat, this time riding in the showjumping ring. Immaculate, determined, somehow familar . . .

"Oh my God!" My eyes flew back to the picture of the medal winners. It wasn't a mistake. It was him. Tall, strong, elegant, his face not yet lined with bitterness; open, positive, ambitious . . . Without the wheelchair.

It was incredible. I used my shaking finger to trace the names at the bottom of the photograph. Jane Kingston on Road Warrior, Mary Underwood on Saint Peter, Beatrice Prescott . . .

I had to read it three times before it sank in. There, right at the very end: Eric Burgess. My heart raced with the very discovery of it. I couldn't stop trembling.

Eric Burgess. *Chef d'équipe*. British Olympic Silver Medal Winning Team. Mexico. 1977.

Eric Burgess had been an Olympic three-day event trainer. So if that was the case, why was he hiding away now?

CHAPTER FOUR

"Her name's Daisy." Mrs Burgess dragged, pushed and cajoled her into the conservatory and then stood for a few moments regaining her composure. "That dog's just uprooted my best rubber plant."

It was easy to see she was Ash's mother: she had the same dazzling blue eyes and black lashes.

"That dog will be the death of us all. It's about time someone got her under control."

Daisy plonked herself down on a welly and visibly scowled.

"Who does she belong to?" I was still smitten despite Mrs Burgess's mud-spattered floor. Daisy obviously wasn't quite the angel she appeared.

"What? Oh, no, never you mind. Just take her back to the stables. Ash will know what to do."

"But if you tell me where to go."

"No honestly, it's very sweet of you, but Ash will sort it out. He always does."

"But . . ."

"Honestly, no buts." Mrs Burgess was looking through a pile of coats for a dog lead.

"But Ash isn't there."

"Oh." She stopped mid-flow. "Oh I see. Well, just leave her in the feed room. If you must know" – she turned round, not quite sure whether to go on, her hand flying up to the pearls round her neck, dithering, fidgeting – "she belongs to someone on the estate. Someone called Eric."

As we went outside, heavy, slow drops of rain were threatening a downpour. "Daisy, come back," I shouted as she barged forward, her ears trailing in a puddle, her face wrinkled in concentration. I turned up my collar and shuddered as a raindrop bounced off a tree and slithered down my neck.

There was something about that house; it was cold, from the inside out. And so many secrets. Why so much covering up about Eric? Why had Mrs Burgess been so reluctant to mention his name? Why had she looked so nervous when she saw me staring at his photograph?

Daisy, on red alert, spotted a rabbit scurrying into its hole and bounded forwards, nearly pulling me off my feet. I felt a swish of water seep up into my boot through a hole in the sole. I started running, galloping along behind Daisy, legs flying forward, memories flooding back from when I was a child and I rode a pretend horse called Phantom. Everybody used to play that game, but somehow my horse used to seem more real. And that's when I felt the first seeds of an idea beginning to form. Only faint at first but then gathering speed. And as the heavens opened and the rain fell in blinding sheets, I knew what I had to do. It was all suddenly so obvious.

*

"Zoe, you'll never guess what I've got to tell . . . Zoe?" I barged into the common room bursting at the seams. There was a note pinned to the dart board.

"Alex, gone home. Fed Barney. See you tomorrow."

The yard was empty. I tied Daisy to the leg of a chair and went to check on Barney and Lace. They were both munching fat hay nets and thought I'd come with extra food. It was nearly six o'clock in the evening. Ash and Judy weren't back with the eventers. The box was still gone and the stables were empty. Chances are they'd stopped off at a pub for something to eat. It had been known for Ash to stay away till eight o'clock if he took the horses on to an indoor school.

This was my big chance. I dived back under the veranda of the main stable block sopping wet and shivering like a puppy. I had to find the courage to go through with it. I couldn't back out now.

There was only one thing to do. I'd have to take Barney – I'd never get there otherwise. The rain was warm: he wouldn't get a chill. Daisy's lead was extendable. All I needed now was the saddle and bridle. My heart was pounding so hard I thought it was going to come through my ribcage. I was all fingers and thumbs, the throat lash wouldn't do up, the girth kept slipping out of my hand. Barney's face was a picture of horror. I don't think he could believe I was asking him to go out in all that rain.

And then Daisy started howling from the tack room. "Barney, whoa, come back." He charged out of the stable with his head stuck up like a giraffe, bristling with excitement and making a beeline for the feed room.

The rain had already soaked his mane and forelock right through and was dripping off his eyelashes. My gloves were sodden and I ripped them off, thinking I'd have a better grip with my bare palms. Daisy poked her head round the feed-room door with the lead caught round her nose like a muzzle. For a hunting dog she didn't seem to care much for bad weather.

"Come on you two, at least give me a bit of support."

Daisy obediently trotted after Barney as I moved off out of the yard. The saddle was wet and my jodhpurs were soaked through within seconds. The reins were greasy and the stirrups all over the place.

"It's all right, Barney." I patted his already drenched neck. "We're going to see Eric."

The farm track round the outside of the wood took forever and I nearly gave up twice. I'd read time and again in newspapers about singers and actors being pushy and pestering producers and directors, driving them crazy in an effort to get recognition, to get to the top.

"He who dares wins," I whispered to Barney, brushing the rain off the brim of my hat. "We've got to believe, it's our only chance."

Daisy chugged along behind, picking out the driest bits. It was turning chilly now, a cold breeze whistling through the trees. The rain had soaked right into the armpits of my oilskin. Barney pulled up and shook himself until my teeth rattled.

"Not much further, boy, I promise." His ears flopped to each side and I knew he didn't believe me.

The rain carried on relentlessly, which seemed to be a message to turn back. I squeezed my heels into Barney's sides and pressed on.

It was half an hour before we came in sight of Eric's cottage, but then we had gone right round the outside of the wood and Daisy had insisted on sitting down every ten minutes for a rest. Now she dashed forward, nearly dragging me out of the saddle, the lead at full length.

"Daisy!"

One of the curtains twitched in the main window. That was really weird. It was still reasonably light but every curtain was drawn. The whole place gave off a feeling of eerie silence. I dropped the lead. Daisy scrambled to the front door and started scratching and whining. There was no response. I slipped down from Barney's back and led him over to some trees where I could tie him up. He stood shivering like a greyhound, all hunched up and sorry for himself. "I'm sorry, boy. Just give me ten minutes."

I turned back to the cottage with determination rising up inside me. Eric Burgess, you might be a stern old man, but I'm not going to take no for an answer.

"Just clear off, go on, clear off, you cheeky girl." He slammed the door right in my face.

"Well thanks a lot," I shouted through the letterbox. "I've brought your dog back and that's the only thanks I get. Well that's just great . . ."

"I never asked you to come up here nosying around," he bawled back through the door. "Now put your brain in gear and get that horse away from those trees before he gets hit by lightning."

He was right, I must have had rocks in my head. "Barney, don't move!"

The reins came undone just as a streak of lightning lit up the sky. "Come on, boy, quick!" I dragged him back to the cottage with desperation starting to set in. "I'm not going until you agree to talk," I yelled at the door, hot tears prickling under my lids. "I don't care if we both get pneumonia."

"Neither do I," Eric shouted back in obvious temper. "Now disappear."

"But your letter . . ." A fresh driving force of rain crashed down from the blackened sky. Barney shook his ears, swished his tail, pulled desperately to go home.

"We can negotiate," I shouted, clutching at straws, feeling my dream starting to fizzle away. "I can pay you for lessons, I can work in your garden."

"Don't you know the meaning of the word no?"

All I knew was that I couldn't give up. Not now I'd come this far. I had to convince him.

The ground was soaking as I sat down cross-legged with Barney standing beside me. I didn't care how long it took: I wasn't going to move, not until that door opened. I'd never felt so cold and wet in my whole life. Barney stared at me as if I'd lost my marbles. My fingers were freezing, my toes wouldn't even wiggle properly.

"OK, OK, I give in." The door opened and Eric glared at me from his wheelchair. "You've got five minutes."

I put Barney in a stable round the back. The oak-beamed cottage was dimly lit; a log fire roared in the fireplace. There were pictures of horses everywhere, ornaments of basset hounds on every available surface, and books lining two walls. It was totally different from the modern estate house I lived in. It was warm, cosy, inviting.

"Well, sit yourself down. Don't look untidy."

I sat on a two-seater sofa, staring across at Daisy who was curled up in an armchair snoring her head off, front paws tucked back like flippers. Eric was in the kitchen which led off from the tiny living room. I could see him manoeuvring himself about, reaching for milk, sugar, everything at waist height. It was unbelievable how he could be so self-sufficient.

I looked away as he came through with a mug

of coffee, his hand trembling, his face a picture of embarrassment. I took the mug and stared up at a picture of him on a huge chestnut hunter.

"How long has it been?" I asked, wanting to swallow the words back as soon as they were out.

Eric's face closed up with pain and he rammed forward to put some extra coal on the fire, hitting the edge of the coffee table.

"You came here to talk about yourself, not me," he barked. "And I don't need the shallow sympathy of a neurotic girl with some heady illusion of being a three-day eventer. Is that clear?"

"Perfectly," I mumbled, looking down at my feet.

"Now here's a towel. Dry your hair off before you catch your death." He threw the towel at me and I suddenly realized I was dripping all over the carpet.

Daisy stirred in her sleep, looked at me with huge droopy eyes and then conked out again. A clock ticked loudly on the mantelpiece. The coal fire flickered lazily.

"Well spit it out, I haven't got all night," he snapped, tapping irritably on the arm of his chair.

"It's about Barney."

"I figured as much."

"I know he's not the best looking pony in the world, or the best behaved."

"Handsome is as handsome does."

"Well, the thing is . . ." Eric's face softened, giving me the strength to carry on. "The thing is,

Mr Burgess, I think he could be a champion. I think he's got what it takes."

The silence was terrible. He didn't say anything. Just sat there rubbing a finger over his chin, thoughtful, waiting for me to carry on.

"I'd better go." I stood up. "I'm wasting my time."

"Sit down and stop being so emotional. If you want something in this life you've got to stick to your guns and go for it, not bottle out. And if you really want my opinion about Barney, I happen to agree with you."

I sat down again, my mouth opening and shutting in shock.

"So will you train us?"

His reaction was not what I expected. He just laughed in my face. He made me feel two inches tall.

"Listen, young lady, I may be confined to a wheelchair now, but I've trained some of the best riders in the world, Olympic medallists. Why would I want to waste my time on a teenage girl who can't even hold the reins properly?"

That hurt, really hurt. How could he be so nasty, so condescending?

"Well, thanks." I stood up, bottom lip quivering. "I might not be a top rider, I might not be good enough for Barney, but at least I'm willing to learn, at least I'm determined to improve, to not be ordinary, to make something of myself. Which is more than I can say for you. You've just given up on life and become bitter. You just sit here and feel sorry for yourself. I know who's the better person."

I was gasping from the sheer passion of it. My voice was heavy. Eric just stared at me, his eyes clear and unreadable. The disappointment was too much to bear. I stumbled for the door, hot tears cascading down my cheeks, my legs light and wobbly. How could he be so horrible? I was a fool to even think . . .

The steady slow clapping started up just as I reached for the latch.

"Bravo, Miss Johnson. That was a fine performance."

"W-what?" I spun round, groping for the back of a chair to keep my balance. "H-how did you know my name?"

"Never mind. What's important is you've just shown spirit and guts, two things every eventer needs by the barrow-load."

I was so shocked that I felt like asking him to run that by me again. His eyes were dancing, lit up by a spark I'd never seen before – in anybody.

"You'll have to be dedicated, follow my rules to the letter, there'll be no messing about."

"No, of course not."

"I'll want you here every day, it won't be easy. Nobody ever got to the top without a bit of sweat."

"Success is ninety per cent perspiration and ten percent inspiration, that's what my mum always says."

"There'll be days when you wish you'd never met me, when you can't move because you ache so much. But there'll be no backing out, you're in for the duration."

I suddenly realized my heart was pounding with excitement. I was perched on the end of the settee already feeling as if I was entered for Badminton.

"My part of the deal is to turn you into a champion."

He reached forward as if to stand up and then fell back in frustration. "Here." He searched for a pen and paper down the side of his chair. In a flamboyant scrawl he wrote something down, tore off the sheet of paper and waved it at me. It simply said today's date – 25th April.

"I give you my word that precisely one year from this moment you'll be a serious contender for the Junior National Team. Is that clear?"

"Yes, sir!" I broke into an almighty grin, then had a sudden thought. "Will you train Zoe as well?"

"If she promises to work hard too. Do we have a deal?"

"You bet we do." I moved over to Daisy and gave her a pat, just something to disguise my brimming emotion.

"Well, let's shake on it then." He held out his hand and I clasped it. For a second our eyes caught and we both knew we were committed. It was as good as any contract.

"Top stuff." Eric leaned back, almost exhausted with his sudden excitement.

I stared into the fire, revelling in the moment, dreaming of the future.

"It's going to be big." Eric turned and smiled at me with a totally different look – a sense of purpose. "There's no time to lose." He smoothed back his hair, already more confident. "Training starts tomorrow!"

CHAPTER FIVE

"It's got to be a secret." I slung Barney's saddle over the stable door.

"But are you sure he's agreed to give me lessons too?" Zoe was standing on a bucket, damping down Lace's cream mane, unable to take in what I was saying.

"Zoe, just tack up Lace. We're late as it is."

I hadn't slept a wink all night. School had been just one long daydream and now I was flying around trying to do my chores and watching the minutes tick by with horrifying speed.

"I still can't understand all this cloak and dagger stuff. Just what is the big deal?" Zoe hadn't shut up all day about the mystery between Ash and Eric. Even in biology she was nattering on about possible swindles, family feuds, even attempted murder.

"Does it really matter?" I said, feeling Barney's leather girth which had set like cardboard after last night's rain. "The most important thing is we've found ourselves a top-class trainer."

"Yeah, well, that's yet to be proven."

"I beg your pardon?"

"Oh come on, Alex, he's a bit of an old has-been."

"And what would you know? Just because he's in a wheelchair?"

"Well yes, no, oh I don't know. But don't tell me you're not dying to find out what's going on. Admit it, Alex, you're as curious as I am."

It took us half an hour to get the horses tacked up and out of the stables. Judy had insisted I scrub out the manger in a spare stable. I'd already filled ten hay nets and tidied up the muck heap. If Zoe hadn't helped I'd have still been there at midnight. Jenny had driven me to despair with a lecture on a special herbal concoction for arthritis, even though Gypsy Fair was as fit as a fiddle. A novice rider with a twitchy grey thoroughbred kept asking me stupid questions like, "What's it called when all four 'paws' stand together?" When I answered "square halt", Zoe started laughing and then had to pretend she'd got an attack of asthma. The only good thing was that Ash Burgess had smiled at me twice and even offered to carry a bucket of water.

"You've got to admit," Zoe said as she watched him school Donavon in the outdoor arena, "he's got the most gorgeous bottom."

The only thing I was interested in was how he managed to do such a perfect collected canter without any apparent effort. Donavon purred round the outside track in perfect harmony with Ash. They dropped down into trot, moved sideways, turned up the centre line and did a perfect pirouette. Just how did he do that?

Judy sauntered across the yard carrying a can

of coke and a martingale and you could smell her perfume a mile off. Ash gave her a megawatt smile, vaulted out of the saddle and led Donavon across to her. I turned around for a split second to watch Reggie and Nigel, the two ducks, pick a fight with a brave wood pigeon. When I turned back Ash had scooped Judy into his arms and was giving her a passionate kiss on the lips.

"Oh, didn't I tell you?" Zoe shot me a half-guilty look. "They've had a thing going for months."

"You're late." Eric wheeled out of the greenhouse, pointedly looking at his watch.

Daisy pottered out behind Eric carrying a tomato cane which wouldn't go through the doorway and Barney started squealing and pushing forward in genuine excitement.

"I think," Eric said, lips pursed with a hint of sarcasm, "we'd better get on, don't you?"

He'd already marked out a dressage arena with some plastic cones on a flat piece of ground at the front of the cottage.

"All I want you to do is walk, trot and canter on the outside track. Let's see how badly you do."

Zoe went first and did quite well with Lace in a nice round shape and doing some good transitions. Barney promptly marched into the arena with his tail swishing and instead of cantering, burst into a volley of bronco bucks which very nearly sent me flying, and then, just when I least expected it, he veered sideways and trampled a cone.

"Well done, Zoe. That wasn't bad at all. Alex, you ride like a jellyfish."

I blushed and I could feel beads of perspiration building up under my crash cap.

"Now let's see you go again."

Half an hour later, after riding without stirrups in sitting trot, I felt as if my body was being torn in half. Zoe was practising canter and doing extremely well. I was beginning to wish I hadn't insisted she have lessons too. Lace was making Barney look like a donkey at the seaside, or worse than that because he couldn't even go in a straight line. I was embarrassed, hot and on the verge of going home.

"OK, enough for now." Eric called us over to him. He was the only one who seemed to be enjoying himself.

"Zoe, you're wooden in the saddle. I want you to do arm swings and neck rolls every morning when you wake up. Alex, you've got weak ankles. I want you to flex them at least twenty times a day and do as many sit-ups as you can – your posture makes a banana look straight."

I don't know whose mouth opened the widest, Zoe's or mine.

"Now come on, let's see what you're like at cross-country."

My stomach was a churning mass of nerves. I honestly thought he was going to ask us to jump all the fences in the parkland. Zoe had turned a mushy pea kind of green and was fiddling frantically with the top of her whip.

Eric refused any help whatsoever with his wheelchair. He methodically and mechanically pumped at the wheels through the rough grassland, his face set in a hard line of determination. Daisy loped after us looking bored but knowing that Eric still had a half-full packet of choc drops in his pocket. Barney sidled sideways feeling as fired-up as a rocket.

"One of the most frightening fences for any cross-country rider is the simple ditch." Eric fought to catch his breath. "Surprisingly, it's not such a big deal to the horse since it has four legs instead of two, but if the rider fusses around on the approach then he's going to muck up."

I was trying to listen but my heart was banging like a steam piston.

"The secret is to ride a straight line, let the horse have a look, and never, under any circumstances, look down yourself. Ride forward, legs on, be positive."

We spent the next half an hour riding over a shallow slope, then a tiny ditch in trot and finally a proper cross-country ditch with a trickle of water in the bottom.

"Look up, look up, legs, legs." Eric seemed to have boundless energy. I felt as if I'd been mauled through a vacuum cleaner. Barney insisted on breaking into canter every time and instead of popping over the ditch nice and quietly, he stuck his head in the air and did a massive cat leap. Eric praised him every jump but said I was even worse than he expected. Zoe was on the sidelines because Eric said Lace wasn't confident enough as yet to tackle a proper ditch. Barney it seemed had enough confidence to jump the side of a house.

"OK, that's enough for today." Eric called us back over to him just as I was about to collapse with exhaustion. I didn't dare ask how we'd done.

"Same time tomorrow. Oh, and half an hour's roadwork before school. Just walking. And Alex, oil your tack, it's a disgrace."

"Just what is he on?" Zoe looked shell-shocked as we started for home. "Is he serious or what?"

Tears were prickling as I caught up with her. I hadn't expected our first lesson to be like that. It was a nightmare.

"Listen, you carry on," I said. "I've forgotten my gloves. I'll meet you back at the yard."

I reined Barney in and turned back to the cottage. Eric was just approaching the front gate as we caught up. "Eric, I mean Mr Burgess, can I have a word?"

He stopped.

"I thought you said we could be champions," I sniffed, feeling weak and defeated. "It's obvious you think we're rubbish." I stood holding Barney's head feeling about to crumble.

Eric gently laughed and fished in his pocket

for a piece of apple. "Enough of that blubbering," he grinned. "I want to admire you, not sympathize with you. And remember, I never said it would be easy."

"But all you did was pick on me. And Zoe just got away with everything."

"Oh poppycock, and stop moaning. How are you ever to improve if I don't criticize?"

"A little encouragement wouldn't go amiss."

"Alex, you're being a wimp. Where's all that fighting spirit? Listen," he went on in exasperation, "Barney is special, I've not changed my mind about that. But he's bored, he needs a challenge. That's why he gets up to all these stupid pranks to amuse himself. You've got to take him by the reins, Alex, and get him to sit up and listen."

"Oh," I said, slumping like a sack of potatoes.

"Don't give me that. You can do it, I know you can. You just need more self-confidence. Here." He rummaged behind his back and brought out an A4 notepad and felt-tip pen.

It seemed he had everything but the kitchen sink stuffed in that wheelchair.

"I want you to take this home and pin it above your bed." He wrote something down in big capital letters and passed it to me. It was just one word: PERSISTENCE.

"If at first you don't succeed."

"Yeah, yeah, I know, try try again."

"Now come on, chin up, straighten that face before the wind changes."

"Yes, sir."

"And if it's any consolation," he said, unwrapping Daisy's lead from round one of the wheels and clipping open the front gate, "when I started to ride, I had the coordination of a three-legged colt. If I can pull myself up by the bootstraps so can you. Now get that horse home before it goes dark."

The radio was playing and the light was on in the common room as I clattered into the yard. Zoe was hosing down Lace's legs and her mother was loading up their Land Rover.

"Alex, can I have a word?" It was Judy.

I trudged into the common room carrying Barney's saddle, my arms leaden with exhaustion. Ash was over by the pool table, his back to me, lining up a shot.

"Alex, we've got a new livery," said Judy. "She's arriving tomorrow after school. I wondered if you could help out?"

Did I really have a choice?

"Apparently she's a friend of yours, or so she says."

"Oh." I shuffled the saddle into a better position. Ash turned round, blank-faced, but obviously interested.

"She's got a really good pony. Wins everything in sight." Judy reached for a chocolate. Only Ash noticed the colour drain from my face. "Her name's Camilla Davies."

50

CHAPTER SIX

"She's awful." I stomped round the stable, attacking a bale of straw with a pitchfork. "I can't even stand being in the same room as her."

"Excuse me." Zoe nibbled a twix bar. "It's as bad for me, you know. We're all in the same year."

Camilla Davies was the most annoying human being I'd ever met. She was also the biggest flirt. If a boy came within a hundred yards of her she'd strut around, batting her eyelashes and flashing her legs.

"She'll have her work cut out with Ash though," said Zoe, watching Judy follow him across the yard like a lovesick puppy.

"I do predict a display of fireworks," I giggled, wondering just how Ash was going to cope with Camilla's advances.

"Speak of the devil," Zoe murmured. "Here she comes."

The Range Rover and matching trailer glided into the yard with a swish of gravel and lots of stomping and wild neighing. Mrs Davies got out dressed in an immaculate oilskin coat and olive-green Hunter wellies.

Camilla looked ready to burst but quickly

regained her composure when she caught sight of us.

"Mummy, you've parked in a puddle." Camilla eased herself out of the door. She was dressed in super-expensive suede jods and a yellow polo-neck jumper which perfectly complemented her ice-blonde hair.

"Doesn't it make you sick?" Zoe mumbled, picking the dirt out of her fingernails. I felt as if my hair hadn't been brushed for a week.

Camilla's pony sounded as if he was going to break out of the trailer at any minute. Judy came rushing across, obviously ticked-off by Ash, and started unhitching the ramp. The aluminium sides were shaking like a leaf.

"He sounds more like a rhinoceros," said Zoe.

We'd heard all about "The Hawk" in daily bulletins from Camilla. How he was bred from an Irish racehorse crossed with a Connemara mare and Mummy had paid thousands for him. He was lean, mean and fast and had won over a hundred rosettes, nearly all firsts, and a table-full of trophies. Camilla went to her first Pony Club event and swept the board.

"Hold him!" The Hawk backed out of the trailer in two bounds, his brown coat dripping in sweat and his tight piggy eyes flicking back and forth like a lizard.

"He's a handful." Zoe shrank back from the flailing hoofs.

"I think he's more fizz than actually dangerous." I stood my ground.

"Oh Alex, what would you know? That pony
of yours was bred from a carthorse," sniped
Camilla.

"Takes one to know one," I lashed back and
stomped off with three empty hay nets. I was furious. How dare she be so rude, and if she thought
I was going to become her own personal slave . . .

"Just let it go." Ash appeared from Donavon's
stable, making me jump out of my skin. "Don't let
her fire you up, she's not worth it." His face was
surprisingly soft. I stepped back a pace and felt my
knees start to tremble.

"Thanks," I gulped and managed a weak
smile.

"Oh and by the way, you've got a piece of
straw stuck to your hair."

"It's Ash!" Camilla was downright embarrass-
ing. She strutted up the yard, swinging her hips,
eyes on red alert. "Camilla Davies," she gushed,
holding out her hand. "I believe you're going to be
giving me lessons." And she smirked with double
meaning. "I think we're going to get on extremely
well, don't you?"

"I'm not interested in any drama that might be
happening in the yard," Eric snapped at Zoe. "The
only thing that matters is what we do here – our
training."

"I thought riding was supposed to be fun," Zoe mumbled under her breath.

"Maybe if you get good at it, it will be," Eric flashed back.

We'd just spent half an hour in the dressage arena doing endless circles and transitions. Apparently I held my inside hand like a concrete post which was why Barney was so stiff through his inside shoulder. Eric insisted I let go of it altogether and just ride with the outside rein and applying loads of inside leg. He was relentless. "Just imagine you're holding a glass of champagne," he chuckled. "You don't want to spill a drop." It didn't stop my hands moving all over the place.

Barney wouldn't settle down until Daisy was positioned at the top end of the arena where he could keep a steady eye on her. He must be the only horse in the country to become best pals with a dog. Daisy, for her part, didn't take a blind bit of notice and happily munched through two sausage rolls which were supposed to be Zoe's lunch and then spent the next half an hour sucking her gums and the ends of her ears.

"No, no, no," said Eric. "You both trot too fast. There's no rhythm. Count out to yourself one thousand, two thousand, three thousand for each stride. Slow, slow, slow."

"One thousand, two thousand, three thousand." Much more of this and my legs were going to drop off for sure. I never knew dressage could be so difficult.

"I can't do it." Zoe threw down her reins in despair when Lace refused to canter on the right leg.

"OK, rest." Eric called us over and offered us both a glucose tablet for energy. "We'll start jumping in precisely ten minutes."

We fixed up some showjumps. Eric insisted on a line of cross poles which had to be exactly equidistant.

"He must be a hermit," Zoe whispered as we climbed back on.

I had to admit it, there didn't seem any other explanation. When we'd arrived at the cottage that day a lady had been coming down the drive and had stopped, stock still, turning white when she saw us. Apparently she was the home help who visited twice a week and she couldn't believe it when we told her Eric was giving us lessons.

"But don't you know?" she had spluttered, eyes wide and still trying to take in what we were saying. "Eric's not had any visitors or even been further than his garden gate for nearly three years . . ."

Eric interrupted my thoughts. "The whole idea of cross poles is to get you jumping straight," he said. "Both these ponies veer to the left, which means in a combination you're going to miss the second and third jumps completely. Now listen carefully: think slow, wait for the fence to come to you. Go off a shorter stride rather than a longer one and look straight ahead. Now off you go."

Barney was dumbfounded. He burst into canter and sprawled over the first jump leaving no room to jump the second, snapped up his forelegs and twisted over the third nearly taking the wing with him.

"That was pathetic." Eric stated the obvious.

"I know, I know, but watch this." I wheeled Barney round, took a firm hold and rode straight and determined. I could feel the mental strength soaring through my veins.

"Perfect!" Eric nearly fell out of his wheelchair.

We finished off by trying to ride a controlled circle after the jumps, varying the direction and pace.

"Keeps the horse thinking," Eric explained. "Keeps him on his toes."

We took Lace and Barney back to the cottage and unsaddled them in the stables while Eric went to put the kettle on. My legs were wobbling as I slithered out of the saddle.

"I don't think I can keep this up," Zoe wailed, collapsing against the wall. "*And* we've got to get up at six o'clock tomorrow to do hillwork before school."

For once Barney didn't butt me in the stomach. He didn't even charge round the stable when I took off his bridle. "You know," Zoe said, noticing the transformation too, "he actually looks happy."

We staggered across the yard, feeling as

parched as a desert and then Zoe clung on to my arm and stared across at the garage. The modern fold-back door was open and there was a small, bright-green car parked inside. There was an orange disabled sticker on the back window.

"If he hasn't been out for three years," said Zoe, her voice sounding like something out of a thriller, "why has he got a brand new car?"

"It's all plugged in to work – you've just got to press the button." Eric passed us mugs of strong tea and reached down for the remote control.

"You mean you've bought this specially?" I looked down at the shiny new video in awe.

"It's about the only piece of new technology which is of any use." Eric opened a video box entitled "Badminton – Ten Years of Glory" and passed it to Zoe. "Now watch, listen and learn."

We all leaned forward round the TV screen with a huge pile of toast dripping in butter and Daisy drooling at the jowls and pushing her cold wet nose against my hands.

There was a brief introduction in front of Badminton House showing the beautiful parkland, and then it was straight into some orchestral music and a famous rider tackling the fences. "Badminton – the most famous three-day event in the world."

I could feel my blood start to tingle.

"More volume." Eric pushed forward, his eyes riveted to the screen. There was a quick shot of

Mary Thompson tackling the water and then another rider going over the famous Whitbread Barrels.

"Mark Todd," Eric said, pointing in excitement. "Probably the best rider in the world. And one of the nicest."

The mouthful of toast stayed stationary, pressed to my gums. I was transfixed. This was where I wanted to be – had to be. One of the youngest riders ever.

"Here, look, this is the bit." Eric started talking us through the next fence, the Vicarage Vee, telling us how it should be ridden.

It was a monstrous post and rail corner with an ugly ditch underneath, about halfway round the course.

"It's big, nasty and testing," Eric butted in over the voice-over.

A big bay horse plunged over, somersaulted and lay sprawled on his side. "Too fast, you idiot." Eric slapped the armrest of his chair in annoyance.

"Here we are, the Badminton lake." A horse was approaching in a zigzag line, all over the place. Eric was totally caught up in the action. "She's gone in too fast. Hold, hold. No, no, no, that's a right pig's ear. Sit back, you stupid fool, sit back!"

Zoe ripped open a packet of biscuits but they never reached her mouth. "That jump is impossible," she gasped.

"That's a tiger trap." Eric pressed the volume

even higher. "Now pay attention. We're coming up to the coffin."

Eric explained that a coffin was a jump in, a stride or a bounce to a ditch and then another stride to a jump out.

Zoe's face had drained pure white. "I won't ask why it's called a coffin," she squeaked.

"We'll start practising that next week." Eric pressed fast-forward.

As the video came to an end, the parting shot was of the famous bronze trophy. I thought I was going to burst with new burgeoning ambition.

"Never could win it." Eric surprised us both. "Went round that course five times but dogged with bad luck. Burghley was always my hunting ground."

I flashed Zoe a look which said "I told you so" and I was never more convinced that Eric knew what he was talking about.

"D-did you ever win Burghley?" Zoe looked at him shyly.

"Oh yes." Eric's face never changed. "Four times to be exact."

He fished in the sideboard and found a folded strip of paper. "This isn't Badminton but it's a start. Take that with you. Study it. Memorize it."

I opened it up and read the bold print in suspense. It was the Pony Club One-Day Event.

"I've already sent in the entries."

Zoe came across and glanced over my shoulder. "But it's only four weeks away!" she said.

"All the more reason to get practising." Eric pressed his hands together.

"But we haven't done a dressage test," Zoe protested.

"I've got no brakes," I wailed.

"We've never done cross-country!"

"Less of the negative and more of the positive," Eric said, putting the video back in its box. "The man who wins is the man who thinks he can. Or in this case young lady."

"But . . ."

"No buts."

"Well, I'm in if you are." I looked at Zoe with anxious excitement, well aware that my hands were shaking.

"Have we got a deal?" Eric smiled at our startled faces. "I want first and second. No less."

I slowly extended my hand and Eric grasped it. Zoe did the same.

"Four weeks." Eric's eyes glistened with the challenge. "And no backing out," he warned. "I want total commitment . . . I want a will to win!"

CHAPTER SEVEN

The headline stood out in bold type:

EVENT RIDER ERIC BURGESS
CRIPPLED IN TRAGIC ACCIDENT
BLAMES NEPHEW

It was at the top of the page. Dated 27th October. Three years ago.

"But it's so tragic," I gasped. "I just can't believe it."

"Neither can I." Zoe peered over my shoulder. "But it's all there in black and white."

While I'd been grooming Barney and Lace, Zoe had been searching through old newspapers at the local library. "I had to find out," she said. "Curiosity was killing me."

Eric Burgess had suffered a broken back after a horrific fall from his favourite eventer, The Brigadier. The horse had a smashed leg and had to be put down on the spot. The accident had happened at a cross-country fence called Lover's Leap. The girth had snapped and Eric had been thrown down a bank with the horse landing on top of him.

All the way through the article Eric was reported to have said "no comment". The whole Burgess family refused to talk and Ash was said to have left the country to join an event yard in Germany. It was one of the grooms who had gone to the papers – a Miss Sandra Brown. She was quoted in the article:

"They were always arguing. Not a day went by when they didn't fight. Mr Burgess was so hard on Ash. In the end Ash started to rebel. He went right off the rails, drinking, refusing to ride. Nobody could do a thing with him. Then Mr Burgess asked him to groom for him at Flushing Meadows. Ash was drunk. The tack should have been checked. There was no surcingle . . ."

"Wow, this is heavy." I had to read the story again just to take it in.

"Mr Burgess banned Ash from the hospital and refused to have anything more to do with him. I think he even took him out of his will."

"Poor Ash," I said, after reading the final paragraph out loud. "Imagine having that on your conscience."

"That's if he cares at all," Zoe said in a small voice. "For heaven's sake, Alex, I don't think they've seen each other for three years."

We agreed not to say a word. It had to be a secret. After all, it was hardly any of our business.

"There's more skeletons in the Burgess cupboard than the whole of this county." Zoe stuffed the photostat sheet into her pocket and did up the zip.

"Yeah, but like we said," I added, "it's none of our business."

The argument started outside the common room. I was leaning on the wheelbarrow feeding an egg and cress sandwich to the two ducks, Nigel and Reggie.

Ash was coming out of the horsebox carrying a bundle of show rugs and Judy ran across the yard to him, obviously crying.

"Well, if you'd calm down I might be able to hear what you've got to say." Ash sounded really irritated.

"She's nothing but a conniving cow." Judy burst into a fresh bout of tears.

By now my ears were straining. I vaguely heard Camilla's name mentioned and wished I'd learnt to lip-read.

"I mean it, I've had enough. I won't be two-timed."

"Stop it!" Ash's voice was dangerously hard.

"You've got to get rid of her, Ash," Judy gulped, mascara escaping in black streaks down her flushed cheeks. "It's either her or me."

The silence was almost unbearable. You could have heard a pin drop. Ash's eyes were narrow and hard. A nerve flickered non-stop in his neck. He turned for the stables, taking measured strides and then swivelled round with a carefully arranged face.

"Judy – *we're finished*!"

"The poor girl." Zoe was astounded. "Who does Ash think he is, a modern day Casanova?"

For the past two weeks we'd been training like demons for the one-day event. My whole body felt as if it had been in a fight with a road digger. I'd nearly fallen asleep at school twice and even the strongest aromatherapy oils did nothing for my aching shoulder muscles. Barney, on the other hand, was glowing and strutted around with his head in the air like a Hollywood superstar.

"If it gets any bigger he'll trip over it," Zoe giggled.

Eric was already waiting by the dressage arena when we arrived. He had his back to us and was stroking Daisy's head. For the thousandth time, my heart went out to him. And now we knew the tragic circumstances of his accident it made it even worse.

"Don't you think, Zoe," I said struggling to contain my emotions, "that life can be really unfair?"

"More leg, Alex. Come on, put your back into it. That transition was enough to put a glutton off his dinner!"

"I think he's actually happy." Zoe rode past on Lace doing a lovely extended trot.

"Don't speak too soon," I grinned. "He's taking notes." Whenever Eric got out his notepad it meant he was jotting down criticisms.

I was riding Barney in a snaffle bit for the first time. Eric explained that the nerve endings in Barney's mouth had become hard and dull which made him so unresponsive. He lowered the snaffle slightly so it was resting on a fresh part of the mouth and suddenly Barney was as light as a feather in my hands. He wasn't even shaking his head.

"Hill work!" Eric bawled out, manoeuvring himself over to the steep slope we'd been using for the past two weeks.

"Slave-driver!" Zoe shouted back, pretending to slump in the saddle with exhaustion.

"If at first you don't succeed . . ."

"Yeah, yeah, we know, try try again."

"Well off you go then. Don't look untidy."

Eric unscrewed the lid of a flask of tea while we took position at the bottom of the slope. Eric swore that battles could be won on sweet tea and was always armed with his tartan flask. Barney loved to slurp up the dregs at the end of the lesson.

We leaned forward and set the horses up the hill in a dead straight line. We were very nearly at the bottom again when disaster struck. Barney was shuffling along, sat back on his haunches and I was just letting the reins filter through my hands.

I really thought we were getting somewhere. I was even beginning to nurture hopes of winning

the one-day event. It never entered my head that
something could go so drastically wrong.

Eric saw the horse and rider first. He froze,
his hand still outstretched passing some chocolate
to Daisy. I'd never seen the colour drain from anybody's face so fast.

Barney started trembling as the horse in front
pawed relentlessly at the ground, chewing on its
bit, wheeling from side to side as the rider nudged
its girth with glossy spurs.

It was Camilla.

"So this is where you've been disappearing
to." She smiled down at us with perfect white
teeth, and then at Eric.

"Do you mind, Camilla." Zoe glared at her
with unexpected ferocity. "We're training. You're
not the only one entering the one-day event."

Camilla burst out laughing. "You're not
serious? You can't be. You don't stand a chance."

Eric looked about to explode. We always
knew he could be rude, but this time he went for
the jugular.

"You don't know what you're talking about,
you stupid airheaded girl." His lips drew back in
a thin pencil line; his voice was barely audible.
"It's quite obvious you haven't got a clue about
horsemanship. Look at you, you're all over the
place."

That must have really stung Camilla because
she gasped and went red.

"I know who you are," she blurted out.

"And I know your secret. Nobody's interested in you. Ash couldn't care less if you rot."

"How dare you," said Eric. There were tears filtering into his eyes. "Get away from me, get away!" He started frantically pushing his wheelchair towards the cottage but his breathing was coming in short gasps. He sounded as if he had asthma.

"Eric!" I leapt off Barney and ran across. He was clutching at his chest and seemed unable to move. "Zoe! Help! I think he's having a heart attack."

Zoe was at my side within seconds, pulling his tie and shirt collar loose. "I – I think he's hyperventilating."

"What does that mean?" I screeched, fear clawing at my own chest until I felt sick.

"It's all right." Zoe read my thoughts. "He's having a panic attack. It'll pass." She bent down and took Eric's hand. "It's all right, Eric, just take deep breaths. Breathe in deep."

Eric sucked in a mouthful of air, gurgled and then let it out again. His hand was clutching on to Zoe's.

"And again."

Gradually his breathing came back to normal. His colour returned and he slumped back in his chair.

"Where on earth did you learn that?" I was reeling from shock.

"My mother used to have attacks all the time,

after she had my baby brother. It got to the stage where she wouldn't go out of the house."

Any more revelations and I thought I was going to go dotty. Camilla had disappeared from sight. Not a trace.

"Let go of me!" Eric pushed away Zoe's hand, fighting desperately to do up his tie. "Leave me alone, both of you. Can't an old man at least hold on to some dignity?" He started pushing at the wheelchair, ramming forward, determined, unrelenting. "We had a deal, Alexandra Johnson. You've broken your word." He carried on towards the house.

"But she followed us," I yelled. "We didn't say a thing. I swear."

He didn't answer.

"Eric!"

He spun round awkwardly, one hand pressing down on the clumsy wheel, clogged up with soil and grass; his face contorted with hurt and betrayal.

"I trusted you. I trusted you both. And all you've done is make me look a fool. Now please, just leave. Go away. Go back to the yard. Go anywhere. But leave me alone!"

CHAPTER EIGHT

Eric refused to answer the door. For three days I banged and shouted and knocked on the windows. But nothing. I even began to think he'd moved out.

Camilla went straight to Ash and blabbed just as we knew she would. It was her mother who had told her about Eric. I kept in hiding and tried to put off the confrontation for as long as possible. Judy was walking around with swollen eyes and a dazed look and kept telling Zoe that Ash couldn't possibly have meant it, that he loved her really.

Ash spent hours in the manege schooling his best horses. He hadn't said a word to anybody since the break-up and just stomped around criticizing everything. He was riding like a fiend. After each hour Judy led out a new horse and he just vaulted straight from one to the other. Poor Judy looked devastated but didn't dare say a word.

"The trouble with this yard," said Zoe, happily demolishing a wedge of cold rubbery pizza, "is there aren't enough men and there are far too many women."

I had to stay behind an extra couple of hours to clean a dressage saddle and two double bridles. Ash had qualified on Donavon for the Young Rider Championships and wanted everything immaculate. The bridles got so mixed up it was beyond a joke and for the life of me I couldn't put them back together. Even worse, my hair trailed in the saddle soap and I ended up smelling like a tack shop.

I was just brushing it out with a clothes brush when Ash suddenly appeared in the doorway. He seemed almost nervous. There was nowhere to bolt for cover so I'd just have to brazen it out. He flung a saddle and bridle up on the rack and started peeling off his gloves. If he didn't speak soon I would die of embarrassment.

"You've got beautiful hair."

I nearly choked. One of the Weymouth bits clattered to the floor and the clothes brush sailed off into the boot bin.

"How's Donavon?" It was the only thing I could think of to say.

Ash had his back to me and was nervously twiddling with a leather girth.

"Listen," he said, turning round and looking acutely embarassed. "I'd like to take you out."

"What, on a hack?" I must have sounded so dim.

"Don't be so silly, I mean on a date." His eyes filled up with such warmth it was like sitting next to a coal fire. My chest was heaving so much I sounded out of breath.

"That would be lov—"

"Of course Camilla told me about Eric, about how you went behind my back." His jaw hardened just a fraction. "And I'm prepared to forgive and forget so long as you—"

"I beg your pardon?" Disbelief mingled with growing fury. "Are you saying that you'll only take me out if I promise to stop having lessons with Eric?"

"Well, yes, that's about the long and the short of it." He leaned against the saddle rack refusing to meet my gaze. I couldn't help noticing the gold watch on his wrist, the taut brown muscular arms, the sleeves of his rugby shirt pushed up and the thick broad shoulders. It made what I had to say next all the more difficult.

"Ash Burgess, you are the most arrogant, pigheaded, stuck-up member of the opposite sex I've ever met!"

I scraped back my chair, scooped up the bits of double bridle and hurled them straight at him.

"Clean your own flaming tack," I fumed, lobbing the tin of saddle soap after the bridles. He ducked just in time as it clunked heavily against a cabinet.

Before he had time to gather his wits I pushed back my hair, marched over to the door, and then swivelled round on my heel. "And just for the record," I said, leaving him in no doubt whatsoever, "I wouldn't go out with you if you were the last man on earth!"

*

"The lady doth protest too much, methinks," Zoe giggled, quoting Hamlet which was one of our set books.

"Zoe, I do not fancy Ash. I never have and I never will."

"Yes darling, whoops, look up there, a flying pig!"

"Zoe!"

"OK, OK, you don't fancy Ash, but tell me why you can't stop talking about him for a second and you've not taken your eyes off Donavon's stable where we both know Master Ash is lurking at this precise moment?"

I was determined to see Eric. I had to talk to him. Had to get him to see sense.

Bluebells formed a rich scented carpet as Barney picked his way through the wood. It was a lovely fresh morning, promising to be a hot day. Barney sparked along, taking long powerful strides. I checked my heels were well down and my shoulders back.

This time I wasn't going to ride straight up to the house. I left Barney tied up to a tree and crept up the back way. It paid off. Eric was in his greenhouse. It immediately brought back memories of when we'd first met, when Barney had dumped me in the flower bed and Eric had given me a ticking-off. So much had happened since then.

A twig snapped under my riding boot. Eric spun round, his hair all over the place and looking shabby for once. "I might have known you'd show up again."

Daisy padded out, delighted to see me, her body weaving like a snake. I gently lowered her huge dirty paws and turned to Eric. "We really need to talk."

The cottage was a mess. Mugs of cold coffee, newspapers strewn across the floor. The television still switched on. It was so unlike Eric.

"Are you all right?" He pushed forward into the kitchen and didn't answer. "Eric, this is stupid. We need you!"

Something about him had changed. He seemed to have aged ten years.

"Nobody needs an old man in a wheelchair." His voice was shattered. "This is all I'm fit for, watching the gogglebox." He turned up the television deliberately to drown out my voice.

"So that's it, is it? You're giving up. What about that golden word 'persistence', or are you just a hypocrite?" I marched across to the television and pulled out the plug. "Eric, are you listening to me?"

He just stared dolefully out of the window.

"You're disabled, Eric, and nothing's going to change that. You either come to terms with it or you sit here and waste your life away. Quite honestly I think you're being selfish and wallowing in self-pity."

"How dare you speak to me like that!"

"Well, somebody's got to! You can't live on bitterness for ever!"

"I'm not bitter, I'm just angry. OK?"

"So hard lines for me and Zoe? So much for the Junior Championships, or was that all hot air? Maybe Camilla's right and Barney and I don't stand a chance."

"Oh, don't be stupid. You've got star quality, girl – it stands out a mile – and so has the horse."

"So why are you turning your back on us?"

"I'm not, I'm just thinking about myself for a change. I'm entitled to do that, aren't I? Go and find yourself a proper trainer, someone who can at least put up the jumps by himself."

"And why would I want another trainer when I've got the best?" I started picking up newspapers and folding them up.

"Leave it, Alex." He waved his arm at the mess. "Please, just respect my wishes and leave me alone."

"We had a deal, Eric. You shook my hand."

"Yeah, well, life never turns out how you expect."

It was useless. I put down the papers and moved towards the door. Daisy watched me with huge sad eyes. It was probably the last time I'd ever see her. I took one last look at the cottage and lifted the latch.

"You know, Eric," I said, hovering in the

doorway, "I never took you for a quitter. Obviously I was wrong."

The door clicked shut and hot angry tears burned in my eyes. Why did life have to be so cruel?

Barney knew immediately I was upset and gently nuzzled my neck as I flung my arms round him. I cried and cried until I felt there were no more tears left to shed. I'd never been more miserable in my life.

"That was our big chance, Barney. Now we're by ourselves. It's just you and me."

I sniffed loudly and he waved back his ears and whickered as if to tell me it would be all right. "You might not be a show horse," I snuffled, leaning down on his neck, "But you're my best friend and I love you to bits."

Back at the yard Judy had Donavon tied up outside the stables and was washing his tail. She had the bucket held right up on her chest, dunking in the long hairs, the water frothy with shampoo.

Donavon was the most beautiful horse I'd ever seen. His bright chestnut coat shone just like a conker. The only marking he had was a white stripe on his head. The total opposite from Barney whose legs and face were murder to keep clean. I'd been washing him even more than usual to keep Eric happy. But that didn't matter any more. Nothing mattered.

I was dying to escape to the common room, wash my face and console myself with three bars of chocolate and a packet of crisps, but Judy was in the mood for a mammoth moan.

I unsaddled Barney and led him across, listening to a stream of abuse about "that nymphet Camilla". If Judy had known about Ash she'd have probably thrown the bucket of water at me.

"So what do you think, Alex, will we get back together?"

I dragged myself into the present and thought about giving her an honest answer. Barney rested his head on my shoulder in total boredom.

Suddenly a tractor came round the corner seemingly at a hundred miles an hour. There was nowhere to move to, nowhere to turn. Barney stood trembling from head to foot, eyes wide with fright, rooted to the spot. Donavon edged sideways straining on his lead rope to see what was going on.

I could almost feel what was about to happen but was powerless to stop it. Everything moved in slow motion. The tractor clattering up to the stables; Donavon moving closer; Barney coiled up like a spring.

"Judy!"

In one quick movement Barney reeled on to his hind legs, crazed with panic, the reins snatching out of my hand. Judy lunged for his head but it was too late. The tractor cut out its engine but seconds too late.

Barney thrummed down on to the ground, wheeled round with amazing speed and cannoned into Donavon's behind. The slicing crash of his hindshoe into Donavon's leg made me wince with shock.

"Oh no!" Judy pummelled Barney out of the way and stood staring at Donavon's near hock in disbelief. Blood was spurting out and a flap of jagged pink skin hung open. "Oh my God, Alex, he'll need stitches!"

I ran after Barney, shaking so hard my teeth were rattling.

"I've got to fetch Ash!" Judy had gone as white as a sheet. Her hands were shaking. "Look after him. He'll need a vet!"

She dived off in the direction of the house leaving me with Barney in one hand and Donavon bleeding and shaking in the other. The man who had been driving the tractor kindly led Barney back to the stable while I tried to comfort Donavon. His neck and flanks had broken into a sweat and he was holding up his hind leg, unable to put any weight on it. What if it was broken? What if he'd chipped a bone? Tears brimmed up to the surface and I clenched my teeth to keep them back.

Ash sprinted into the yard, his face a picture of cold fury. "What the hell have you done?"

He took one look at Donavon's leg and rounded on me like a wild animal. His voice was glacial.

"You've ruined him." He sounded at breaking point. "You've screwed up all my chances."

"It wasn't my fault," I croaked, my voice starting to crack.

"Don't tell me it was an accident?"

"Of course it was. You don't think Barney did this on purpose?" My head was beginning to throb. My back was aching. "Maybe it looks worse than it actually is."

"What?" Ash gave me a thunderous look. "At worst he'll be crippled. At the very best he'll be off work for two months. There's a boy, whoa now, nobody's going to hurt you. Have you any idea what this is going to do to my career?"

I offered to pay the vet bill.

"Do you think that's going to make the slightest bit of difference?" I thought he was going to hurl something at me. "I want you and that nag of yours out of here." He was shaking with anger now. "You've got one week. And then I never want to see you again. Do you hear? I never want to see you or that stupid horse ever again!"

CHAPTER NINE

"He was angry. He'll get over it," Zoe said, looking doubtful.

I think we both knew it was a lost cause. "I don't know what to do. I don't know where we're going to go!"

Panic was setting in and fast. The deadline was tomorrow and I still hadn't found anywhere to put Barney. All the livery yards were full and the one riding school that did have a spare stable had heard about Barney's reputation. "It's not his fault he's scared of lorries and tractors," I begged down the phone. "He was nearly killed on a motorway."

"There's got to be somewhere." Zoe scoured the Horses and Ponies column in the local paper.

"At this rate I'll have to put him in our back garden." I felt like screaming out in frustration. "How could Ash do this to me?"

Donavon was confined to his stable but nothing was broken. The vet said it would heal OK but Ash would miss the Young Rider Championships. The one-day event was on Saturday but that seemed a million miles away. Neither of us had heard from Eric and suddenly being an eventer seemed an impossibility, an unrealistic dream. The only reason I hadn't torn up my entry number was because I'd decided to pin it up in my bedroom as a reminder of what could have been.

Barney sank into deep depression and wouldn't touch a scrap of food.

"I think he's missing Daisy," I said, stroking his neck.

"Either that or he's turning anorexic," Zoe answered.

"It's so depressing," I said. "I really thought we were going to be champions."

Camilla was parading around like the cat who'd got the cream. The Hawk was looking fantastic and jumping three-foot-six spreads in the manege. The result of the one-day event was a foregone conclusion. And as for Ash, she was welcome to him.

"I always said he was too much for you," twittered Camilla like an aggravating canary. "There's no way Barmy Barney would have got round that course. He'd have been out of his class. I'm only saying this so you don't make a fool of yourself."

"Oh go boil your head, Camilla. What would you know?" I stomped off in a mood and tried to take my mind off horse homelessness by helping Jenny put a poultice on Gypsy Fair. The big soft mare held up her foreleg like a dog's paw and loved every minute of it.

I was going to miss this yard. The owners, the excitement, Ash's eventers, even Camilla's barbed comments. At least there was never a dull moment. All I'd got to look forward to now was having Barney cooped up lonely in a desolate field, and that was at best.

I swept away a streak of tears and tried to be more positive. But that made me think of Eric and I ended up even more miserable. Judy tried her best to think of solutions but there was no way she'd put in a good word with Ash and that's what I desperately needed. Pride had gone out of the window. I'd beg if I had to.

Fortunately or unfortunately I didn't get the chance. That afternoon Ash disappeared with Judy and three of the novice horses to a local hunter trial with the specific instructions that I was to keep an eye on the yard. I was still working off my last week's livery charges and the other groom had taken the afternoon off to go to the hairdresser's.

It was just me, Barney, the other horses and a flask of tomato soup. I spread out Barney's rug in the corner of the stable and curled up inside. There was something comforting about sitting in a stable listening to horses munching away at hay nets. Barney had a doze with his bottom lip hanging and then shuffled round to sniff at my feet.

I must have dozed off because when I woke I was curled up in a tight ball and the other horses were banging at their doors with an urgent need to be fed.

"What is it, boy, what's the matter?" Barney

was nudging my arm and then marching over to the door, looking out with strained eyes and then coming back and whickering, pawing at the straw until the concrete floor showed through. "Barney?"

For a minute I thought he had colic and then I decided he must be hungry. Then I heard the desperate scrabbling of hoofs on brick walls and my blood drained down to my boots.

It was coming from Donavon's stable. "Oh please, don't let it be what I think it is."

I yanked open Donavon's door, already convinced of the worst. There he was, lying at the back of the stable, thrashing around with his off fore and hind legs trapped against the wall. It was the first time I'd seen it in real life and all the advice of dozens of horse manuals deserted me. Donavon was cast and I didn't have a clue what to do.

It usually happened when a horse got down to roll and literally became stuck against the wall. It usually happened to big horses who were always rolling. It was then that I saw Donavon's anti-cast roller slung in the corner next to the manger. Somebody had forgotten to put it on.

Help. There wasn't a soul in the yard. Come on girl, think, think, what to do? Panic was rushing through my body at a hundred miles an hour. Only the other day I'd read about a racehorse who'd got cast and twisted his gut. The result was fatal. This was serious – Donavon could die!

I charged into the common room towards the

telephone. The vet's number was pinned up on the noticeboard in case of emergencies. I almost instinctively dialled 999 and then changed it to the code and six digit number. My hands were clattering all over the place.

"Hello, Dalton Veterinary Hospital. Can I help you?"

"Yes." My voice came out in a rush. "It's – it's an emergency!"

Both vets were out on other calls. "Just try to stay calm, Miss Johnson. Someone will be with you as soon as possible."

What good would that do! Donavon was a whisker away from losing his life and a receptionist was asking me to stay calm.

I dived back to the stable hoping by some miracle Donavon was back on his feet. He wasn't. His legs and body looked painfully crunched up and his usually placid eyes were oozing fear. The sweat was running off him in rivulets. "It's all right, boy. I'll get you out of this. You've just got to hang on."

But all my soothing words did was cause him to struggle more. If it was a human you could explain to them why it was vital to stay still. How did you stop a horse from panicking and potentially breaking a leg?

"Steady, Donavon. Just hold still!"

I raced back to the common room and stared at the phone. I didn't have a choice. I'd have to do it.

I tapped out the number at breakneck speed. 695124. "Come on, come on, please answer the phone." I heard ringing. One, two, five times. No answer. "Don't do this to me!"

I put it down and then rang again. This time somebody answered.

"*Eric!* It's Alex, something terrible's happened!"

He talked me through it on the phone. "But I can't do it by myself," I pleaded. "There's nobody else here. There's nobody at the house either. Eric, I need you!"

He told me where to get the ropes, then said, "Listen, keep him calm. Don't leave him . . . I'm on my way!"

I stood in Donavon's stable talking to him constantly and pleading with him to stay still. I told him about how I'd first got Barney and how if he was really good I'd bring him a piece of Barney's favourite flapjack. I even started singing lullabies but I could only remember half the words and my voice sounded terrible.

It seemed as if a lifetime dragged by and nobody came anywhere near. Of all the times for the yard to be empty it had to be now.

The green Fiesta spluttered up the drive at ten miles an hour. Relief and shock nearly knocked me off my feet. I thought Eric would ring someone for a lift or get a taxi. I didn't expect this. His face was close to the windscreen, grey as stone and utterly petrified.

I ran out to help him with the wheelchair but he waved me back. "Stay with the horse," he yelled. "Don't let him struggle."

I turned back into the stable, letting Eric get out of the car. He needed to do it himself – for his own self-respect.

"Have you got the ropes? Good, that's just the ticket. I hope you're strong, Alex, because this usually takes two strapping men. Not one man in a wheelchair and an adolescent girl." His voice was suddenly back to normal. He was rising to the challenge.

"We'll find the strength," I said, drawing on his courage. "We've got to."

Donavon lay with his head pressed back on the straw. All the fight seemed to have gone out of him. I tied the two ropes to each of his trapped legs as quickly as I could, just as Eric said.

"Good, good. Now stand back. Watch those hoofs when he comes up. I don't want to have to take you to hospital. After three, when I say, pull firm and steady."

We each took hold of a rope. Donavon watched with wild and panic-stricken eyes. "It's all right, boy. It'll soon be over."

I knew Eric wasn't telling me the risks, what could go wrong.

"Brace your knees," he said. "One, two, three."

The rope tore into the soft flesh of my hands. Eric's face was going purple with effort. Donavon started squealing in panic. The rope was coming loose, it was slipping off Donavon's hind leg.

I didn't think straight. I moved forward towards him, towards the thrashing legs.

"Alex!"

The hoof sent me flying before I could step aside. It knocked me back across the stable and into the wall. Stars swirled in my head. I felt my mouth filling up with warm blood and something else, a shattered tooth all over my tongue.

Eric looked terrified. I couldn't talk for the knife-grinding pain. It felt as if my whole mouth was on fire.

"Alex?"

"It's all right," I finally managed to croak, blood pouring out as I opened my mouth. "Let's try again." I leant back against the wall in a fog of dizziness. "If at first you don't succeed . . ."

We got the rope back on the leg. This time Donavon was quieter. Resigned to whatever we might do.

"This is it." Eric tightened his grip. "Pull! Pull him over!"

He came up in a flurry of flashing legs but this time we were both well back, pinned at the side of the manger.

"Good boy." Eric was ecstatic. "Fantastic, wonderful clever boy."

I tried to smile and felt my face crack with pain. My lips were swelling up like balloons.

Donavon stood trembling, relieved, his head down between his knees.

"He's all right," Eric said, glancing over him with an expert eye. "No serious damage."

"I'll be the judge of that." A friendly face appeared over the door. "Jack Douglas. Veterinary. But it looks as if I'm too late."

"You're a very brave girl." Mr Douglas satisfied himself by cleaning up my mouth and dousing me in antiseptic which stung like mad. "I don't think you'll be very happy when you look in the mirror though."

"I know," I said, running my tongue tenderly over the gaping hole. "I've lost a front tooth!"

I sat down on a bale of straw, the shock and pain only just beginning to set in. Eric talked to the vet and I gently lowered my head between my knees.

The horsebox crunched up the drive just as the vet was about to pull away. Judy jumped out, clutching a handful of red rosettes and Ash, seeing Jack Douglas, immediately looked alarmed. Even more so when his eyes settled on Eric. "What? What's happened?"

He looked down at me, curled up on a straw bale. "You were supposed to be in charge." My head was thundering like thirty galloping race-horses and I didn't need a lecture from Ash. I bent down lower and groaned. He couldn't see my face.

"And why wasn't his anti-cast roller on? Do you realize he could have died?"

I didn't have the energy to tell him he'd been the last person in Donavon's stable. All I wanted to do was go to sleep.

Eric's voice blasted out like an army officer. "Leave the girl alone. She saved your horse's life, for goodness' sake. She deserves a medal, not a dressing down."

I vaguely saw Ash, stunned for words, staring at his uncle, his eyes flooding with mixed-up emotions.

Eric reversed his wheelchair, softening a little, taking in the profile of his long-lost nephew. "I think it's time you and I had a talk."

CHAPTER TEN

"Well, if nothing else I've brought them back together," I mumbled, frozen up with dentist's anaesthetic and my jaw like cardboard.

Eric and Ash had buried the hatchet. They'd spent hours locked in the common room and when they came out Ash offered to drive Eric home. They both looked as if a ten-ton weight had been lifted off their shoulders.

"I wish I could say the same for you." Zoe eyed me beadily and put a hand on my forehead. "You look terrible."

My bottom lip, nose and chin were red, sore and swollen and I was still missing a front tooth. All day at school I'd tried not to smile and if I did have to talk I kept one hand over my mouth. But by lunchtime everybody was calling me gappy and the toothless wonder. The dentist couldn't fix it up until next week. He'd just given me an examination and something to take away the pain.

I felt so miserable I was dragging myself around like a lame dog. This was the last day of Ash's deadline and I still hadn't found anywhere to put Barney. My parents had even suggested I might have to sell him. I just wanted the ground to open up and swallow me. I'd had enough.

"Here he comes," Zoe said, looking through the common-room window. "He's coming straight this way!"

Ash loomed in the doorway blocking out all the light and staring at me.

"I think I'll check Lace's hay net." Zoe made a rapid getaway.

I hung my head and waited for the worse.

"You're right." Ash marched across and pulled up a chair opposite me, his long legs sprawling out and touching mine. "I have been arrogant, pig-headed and stuck-up and I deserve to lose you for ever."

"W-wha." I tried to talk and gave up.

"You poor thing." He gently raised a finger and touched my cheek. "At least now I can talk without you constantly butting in."

I started trembling and wondered if this was some kind of hallucination.

"Of course you don't have to move Barney," he went on, talking more than he'd ever done before. "I've behaved like an utter pig and it's no wonder you hate me."

For one wonderful moment I thought he was going to take hold of my hand. "It's just that you're so beautiful, when I first saw you it blew me away."

"Uh, oo, I . . ."

I was so happy I felt as if I was flying.

"When I saw you sitting on that straw bale with blood all over your shirt I was panic-stricken.

I thought you were hurt, but all I could do was rant and rave."

He leaned closer and stared into my eyes until I had to lower my lashes. "I know you don't fancy me, and that's what made me so grouchy and angry, but do you think, possibly, we could be friends?"

His eyes filled with such softness and concern I could have happily fainted.

"Oh, Alex." He leant closer and I could see his perfectly shaped mouth moving in to kiss me.

I suddenly remembered my missing tooth.

"No!" I leapt up, panic-stricken and bolted out of the door like a startled deer. It was only when I reached Barney's stable that I stopped and listened to my heart thumping like a steam train and a voice hammering in my head. I'd just behaved like a prize dork. I'd been so stupid! A cloud of gloom settled over me. This time I really had blown it for good.

Eric had left a message that he wanted to see me. He'd rung the yard and spoken to Judy. At least it was something. Maybe, just maybe, there was a glimmer of hope that he'd changed his mind. Zoe begged me not to get my hopes up but I threw on Barney's saddle and bridle and set off at a pounding trot.

Daisy was stretched out on the lawn when I arrived. Barney whickered with joy and bulldozed up to her, lowering his head so she could lick his nose.

"It's obvious I'm second best in his books." Eric emerged from behind a flower bed holding a pair of shears.

He was really smart in a shirt and tie and tweed jacket.

"You look a worse mess that I thought," he said, examining my face.

"Thanks," I tried to mumble.

"Remember this flower bed?" He dead-headed a yellow chrysanthemum and put it in his pocket.

How could I forget? That was the exact place Barney had dumped me and I'd first met Eric.

"Nice horse you've got there." He backed up and looked Barney up and down just like he'd done on that first fateful day. "The tack's filthy. And his tail needs washing." Eric squinted his eyes. "He could go a long way. It's a pity the rider gives up at the first hurdle."

He winked at me as I turned in surprise. Slowly, like a crumpled leaf unfolding, I broke into a huge, steady grin.

Eric whipped out his notepad and started giving out orders. "Six o'clock start tomorrow morning," he said. "Zoe's dressage is at 9.30. You're in at ten o'clock. I want that pony washed, plaited and fed by 8.30 and you looking half decent by nine. Is that clear?" He tried to look stern but his eyes were twinkling.

"Oh and I nearly forgot." He threw two cross-country shirts at me that he had stuffed behind his back. They were green with a white flash.

"I've had them specially made up. They were my colours. I figured they might bring you both luck."

I was so touched I ran forward and gave him a big hug.

"Now don't get all soppy." He looked embarrassed but happy. "There's work to be done. Get back to the yard and get Barney cleaned up. I want him to look the best on the field."

I put my foot into the stirrup and swung into the saddle, shoving the shirts inside my jacket and zipping it up.

"Oh and Alex?"

I turned Barney round.

"Thanks. Thanks for giving me back my spirit, a reason to go on. I couldn't have done it without you."

"We're going to be late!" I squealed as Barney stood on the plaiting thread and the nylon stocking protecting his tail started a downward slide. His legs had turned a dishwater grey overnight and there was a big black stain on his nose from heaven knows where.

"Zoe, please, have mercy!" Lace was looking a picture of beauty and elegance and Zoe had already got her rugged and bandaged up.

"Help," I groaned as another neat rosebud

plait popped open. I attacked it with the hairspray and then followed Judy's advice and daubed them all in glycerine.

"He'll need surgery to get those out," Zoe giggled as I gave my own hair the same treatment.

A frenzy of activity was coming from The Hawk's stable and then the door burst open and he plunged out in colour-coordinated rugs and bandages and a head collar with a sheepskin noseband.

"Talk about posing," Zoe tutted. "*And* she must have used a trowel to put all her make-up on."

"More like a cement mixer," I growled, stabbing myself with the needle and then deciding I needed the loo for the fifth time.

"Here's the trailer!" Zoe's mother zoomed into the yard looking hot and flustered.

"Yes, but where's Eric?"

Barney and Lace went into the trailer first time which is more than could be said for The Hawk who had to have the hosepipe sprayed at him.

"Alex, will you please stop fussing and just get in the car."

It was half an hour's journey to the showground and we were supposed to be taking the scenic route but somehow ended up on the main dual carriageway. Lorries hurtled past in the fast lane and we could feel the trailer wafting from side to side. Barney would be going out of his mind.

"How much longer?" I asked, feeling my stomach doing gymnastics.

Barney started stamping in the back.

"Why are we slowing down?" I asked, panic creeping up on me. Zoe was frantically arranging her hairnet in the interior mirror.

"I don't believe it." Mrs Jackson clutched the steering wheel, pumping the accelerator and staring hopelessly at the petrol gauge. "I hate to say this, but I think we've run out of petrol."

We pulled over on to the verge and switched on the hazard lights. I leapt out to check on Barney who was shaking like a leaf. Lorries rattled past without a single thought for three stranded women.

"Oh dear." Mrs Jackson was fast going to pieces. "The mobile phone's in your dad's briefcase!"

I thought it couldn't get any worse. But then Camilla's Range Rover and trailer purred past and we decided it definitely could. We were just debating whether there were any telephones on dual carriageways when a police car pulled in behind us and two officers got out.

It took seconds to ring the stables and speak to Judy. "Don't worry," she insisted. "I'll sort something out!"

Meanwhile, the police officers were arranging cones around the trailer and passing cars were slowing down with little kiddies staring out of the back windows.

"I'm supposed to be doing my test in thirty-five minutes." Zoe was beside herself. "It's hopeless, Alex. We're not going to get there. It's all been a waste of time, all that training . . ."

Even the police officers were shocked when they saw the huge horsebox flashing its lights and pulling in behind us. It was cream with a red streak and an extremely good-looking man behind the wheel.

"I don't believe it," said Mrs Jackson. "It's Ash Burgess!"

While the police held up the traffic, we quickly hurried the horses up the massive rubber-matted ramp and came out through the living quarters and the groom's door. Mrs Jackson and Ash threw in all the tack.

"Talk about making a grand entrance." Zoe climbed up into the monstrous cab.

Ash released the handbrake and eased out into the traffic. Two horseboxes fell into line behind us and a car and trailer in front.

"OK." Ash moved the gearstick and gave me a heartwarming smile. "Let's get this show on the road!"

It was every girl's dream, pulling on to the showground in a sponsored horsebox. Horses and riders were diving all over the place. The loudspeaker was blaring out; there were queues of people at the burger stall and at the toilets. But everybody stopped and stared at Ash.

Zoe raced off to the secretary's tent while I tested my legs and silently admitted I was scared stiff. Ash was already unloading Lace. I scoured the car park for a green Fiesta. Zoe came flying back clutching two black and white numbers, her hairnet falling off. She looked at me. "What's the matter, Alex?"

"It's Eric," I said, my voice leaden with panic. "He's not here!"

CHAPTER ELEVEN

"Number 16. Zoe Jackson on Midnight Lace." The loudspeaker was daunting. The dressage was running half an hour behind schedule.

"Good luck," I hissed as Zoe rode into the arena at Marker A.

Barney butted me in the back and then tried to chase after a pretty Welsh mare.

"Where *is* Eric?" I turned round to speak to Ash.

"What?" Instead I came face to face with Camilla. "Ash left five minutes ago. Look, there goes the horsebox now."

My stomach sank. First Eric. Now Ash.

"He obviously doesn't care as much as you thought." Camilla couldn't resist a smirk.

The Hawk glared at Barney with such venom I thought he was going to attack us.

"Good luck, Alex." Camilla dug in her spurs to move off. "I really think you're going to need it."

Zoe did a fantastic test. She rode out of the arena on a loose rein, grinning from ear to ear, her freckles shining. "She was brilliant," she shrieked. "Did you see that figure of eight?"

I tried to work Barney in but he was already

boiling over. He did six bucks in succession and then backed into a bristly cob and caught the bumper on a Mercedes estate.

Everything was going disastrously wrong. Where was Daisy? Eric promised. All that training. I tried to get a grip but it was hopeless. Barney was getting worse by the minute. Two lads sprawled on a horsebox ramp wolf-whistled and lobbed an empty crisp packet. "What's that, a horse or a donkey?"

I had to keep my cool. I had to.

"Number 27. Alexandra Johnson."

I trotted up the centre line and did a square halt which was quite impressive. Maybe Barney was going to concentrate after all.

I was just about to move off when Barney backed up a step and started to spread his legs. A crowd of spectators burst out laughing and the judges in the caravan in front stared in horror. Oh Barney, how could you do this to me?

He was going to the toilet! I gingerly stood up in the saddle and waited until he'd finished, my whole face bright red. I'd never been so embarrassed in my whole life.

Somehow we managed to get through the test without taking a wrong turn. But then I got a fly in my eye and couldn't see Marker E to move into canter. Barney waltzed out of the arena extremely pleased with himself and I just wanted to go behind the nearest horsebox and cry my eyes out.

"It wasn't that bad." Zoe tried to cheer me up.

"Oh no, it wasn't bad," I said, wanting to scream. "It was terrible!"

We both had a hot dog with double helpings of onions and browsed past the saddlery tents still leading the horses. Zoe insisted that it could only get better but I wasn't convinced. The only saving grace was that most people were messing up the dressage. One boy on a sprung-up thoroughbred had even bolted out of the arena.

The showjumping course was massive. I nearly fainted on the spot. Zoe went pale. "I can't jump those! I can't even see over the top of them!"

Two girls in extra-tight jodhpurs joggled out of the arena with equally tight scared faces. Everybody was whispering and nudging elbows. One dad even produced a tape measure and slapped it against the red brick wall. Every single jump looked the maximum height.

"I think I need the loo." Zoe flung Lace's reins at me and charged off to the ladies' tent only to find a thirty-foot queue and somebody desperately trying to peg down the escaping canvas.

I was just about to consider pulling out, retiring while I was still in one piece, when a familiar voice boomed out behind me.

"Alex Johnson, don't tell me you've lost your nerve."

It was Judy. She strode across like a true professional loaded up with back protectors, brushing boots, crops and jockey skulls. "Ash sent me," she explained.

I'd never been so glad to see a friendly face.

"He's gone off to see Eric," she said, her face dropping ever so slightly. "I'm sorry, Alex, but I don't think he's coming."

My heart seemed to turn into a huge heavy stone. How could Eric let us down like this, just when we needed him most? "Well, Eric can please himself," I grunted, desperately trying to hide my disappointment. "We'll just have to cope without him."

"You can do it, Alex. Just hold him together." Judy had taken over as trainer, standing in the collecting ring, sunglasses propped in her hair, stopwatch round her neck. All the dads were watching her, much to the annoyance of the mums. We'd completely taken over the practice jumps. "Legs, legs, remember to keep a rhythm."

The last three competitors had crashed through the final combination.

"Keep on a short stride," Judy shouted after Zoe.

Lace got ten faults. Camilla went in straight after and did a perfect clear.

"Alexandra Johnson. Number 27."

My legs dribbled away to jelly as I waited for the bell. I think I jumped most of the fences with my eyes closed. It was only when I dismounted and loosened the girth that I realized what we'd done. Zoe was shaking me by the shoulders. "You've got a clear round!"

But it looked as if it might not count. Judy came running back from the secretary's tent with the news. The whole event might be called off. Competitors were complaining left, right and centre about the cross-country course. Apparently it was monstrous and far too technical, and a third of our class had already withdrawn.

I nervously led Barney up and down, readjusting his sweat rug. Zoe had been to look at the scoreboard. "If it goes ahead," she whispered, "you're in with a real chance."

Judy held the horses while we walked the course.

The coffin was steep, deep and lethal.

"Never mind about wanting to go to Badminton," Zoe squeaked. "I think we're already here."

The rest of the fences were just as bad. From complicated twists and turns to unforgiving solid fences. There was a bounce to a bank which looked unjumpable and I was particularly worried about the table which was the final fence.

Mrs Brayfield, the Pony Club Secretary, looked worried as she strutted over to the commentator's caravan. Zoe squeezed my hand.

"I am pleased to announce that this year's one-day event will go ahead as planned."

"Yes!"

The bounce to the bank had been disqualifed, but the coffin and the table still stood. Mentally I went through every fence until I could picture my exact line. Eric's voice was in my head like a guardian angel. "Do your homework – know the course like the back of your hand. Know every blade of grass."

I tightened Barney's girth and prepared to mount. Zoe was one of the first riders to go – a pathfinder. Lace looked surprisingly relaxed and I had every faith. I pulled down the collar on my cross-country shirt and gritted my teeth. We were going to do this and we were going to do it well.

The first clutch of riders didn't even get halfway round. Zoe's confidence was buckling fast. "Just go for it," I yelled.

"Three. Two. One. Good luck." The starter sent her on her way and the last I saw was her bobbing over the log into the wood.

Barney was unusually lethargic. He seemed really tired, or was it just depression? A beagle walked past on a lead and for a second I could swear he thought it was Daisy. Judy passed me a can of coke but my stomach was churning like a washing machine. A heavy black cob came limping back over the finish line with his nose and neck covered in dust.

"Oh God, Judy, I don't think I can do this!"

Camilla trotted over to the start. The Hawk was wound up like a crazed racehorse. The hair on his neck and between his hind legs was lathered white with sweat. "Three, two, one – go!" He shot off like a bullet and leapt the first fence two strides out.

We strained to hear the commentary but it was so crackly. Lace had had a first refusal at the coffin. We couldn't see a thing. I crossed my fingers.

"Number 27, you're in next." I couldn't face it. I couldn't do it.

"Here she is!"

Zoe thundered over the finish line, bent low over Lace's neck. "We did it," she shrieked. "We got round!"

Judy grabbed the sponge and water and raced across to Lace.

"Number 27, be ready."

I couldn't even feel my hands on the reins. There was something wrong with Barney – he didn't feel right.

"Wait!" I'd have recognized that voice anywhere. Suddenly a long low howl rent across the course and I knew it was Daisy. Eric was here!

Barney's ears shot forward and he immediately came to life. I swivelled my neck round to see Ash pushing Eric's wheelchair, Daisy bounding forward on an extendable lead, Eric waving a bowler hat.

"Number 27!"

I tightened my reins and felt the adrenalin surge through my veins. Daisy pushed her nose into Barney's and he squealed in delight.

"Watch the coffin," Eric said, breathless. "Go

in steady, they've all been taking it too fast and falling."

"Don't push too hard up the hill," Ash added. "You'll lose too much energy."

"Number 19, The Hawk and Miss Camilla Davies have retired," the loudspeaker peeled out.

This is it, Alex. This is your big chance.

"Three. Two. One." The starter brought down his arm. "Go!"

Barney bounded forward.

"Whoa boy, steady." We cleared the first and second fences. He was with me every stride, using his head, giving it all he'd got. "Good boy, come on now." He took the stone wall, then the hedge, turn back for the straw bales. The coffin loomed ahead. "Steady, steady!"

I managed to prop him back on his hocks but he was fighting; I couldn't see a stride. He went in too fast but checked himself in the nick of time. Clear!

"That's my boy." We powered on with amazing speed. He was giving me the ride of my life. The water came and went, a rising spray drenching my face. I vaguely remembered seeing spectators gasp. But it was just me and Barney – and the fences ahead.

The open ditch, turn left, up the hill to the log, down the other side to the tyres, the tiger trap. Barney stumbled slightly, recovered in a flash and put in a massive leap. I was exhausted now, every muscle aching, but I kept on riding, hanging in there.

The table was the only fence left. It was maximum height, built like a picnic table with a bench on the take-off side. And it was wide. We had to meet it just right.

"Whoa, boy." I could feel him tiring. He'd given so much, I just needed one more effort.

We slowed down, checked, pushed forward. I had the perfect stride. My hands moved forward ready for take-off. The crowd was ten deep.

Suddenly a red balloon drifted across straight in front of the fence. For one blinding moment I froze in panic. Then Barney veered to the right and I lost my stirrup. All I could do was hang on and pray. We were too far away, we'd never make the width.

Barney lunged forwards and upwards, grunting with the effort. He'd never do it. I clung on to his mane with one hand and let the reins slide through my fingers with the other. I could almost feel his mind working like a computer.

There was a huge gasp from the crowds. Barney had banked the table! There he was, all four legs standing on the top, quivering as he judged the take-off. I opened my eyes to see the ground swirling down below. It was like looking over the edge of a cliff.

"Go on, boy, go on." I gave him his head and he cat-leapt off.

"Lean back!" Eric's words echoed in my head.

We were coming down too steep. We were going to fall!

With the skill of a real champion, Barney scrabbled for a foothold, his neck snaking down almost to the ground. Then he came back up, propping me half into the saddle, his legs surging forwards, looking for the finish line, doing it all himself.

"Hold on, Alex," someone shouted from the ropes. It sounded like Eric.

I wrapped my arms round Barney's neck and clung on for dear life.

"You've done it!" Zoe came running up, patting Barney like mad. The next thing I knew Ash was pulling me out of the saddle, lowering me to the ground, and then taking a firm hold as I rocked and swayed.

"Any drama and you're at the centre of it," he laughed.

"At least I haven't lost any more teeth," I quipped and then turned and buried my head in Barney's neck, tears of relief and overwhelming pride flowing freely.

"I always knew that horse was special." Eric's voice filtered over everybody else's. Daisy plodded across and stuck a big paw on my riding boot.

"We did it, Daisy. We showed them."

Zoe and Judy took off the saddle and sponged Barney down while I tried to recover as well as savour the moment. People kept coming up and saying "great round" and "cracking horse". One man in a tweed hat offered a telephone number and his business card in case I wanted to sell him.

"Never," I answered without a flicker of hesitation.

The newspaper photographer pushed his way in. "Smile, everybody."

"Oh no," I grinned. "I look awful."

"She's already getting vain," Zoe said.

"Stardom's going to her head," Eric tutted.

"When's the prizegiving?" Ash looked around.

"But what about banking the table – won't I be eliminated?"

"Definitely not." Eric gave Barney more mints. "It's well within the rules."

Ash was fuming about the table being on the course at all. "Don't they know that having a table as the last jump is downright dangerous?"

I knew for a fact that one of his eventer friends had been killed at one when his horse took off too close and somersaulted. At the end of a course, tables are just too difficult for a tired horse to cope with. Eric vowed to put a formal complaint in writing and also to warn against selling balloons at horse events. "It was just plain irresponsible. Alex could have been killed."

"I think you've won." Judy took Barney's reins so she could lead him round to cool off.

Zoe and I bolted over to the horsebox to change into our showjumping jackets and black hats. It was the done thing to look smart at the prizegiving. I still couldn't believe that I was in with a chance. I pulled on my white gloves and jumped out of the groom's door.

"Don't you feel really special?" Zoe looked up at the beautiful cream horsebox and beamed from ear to ear. Lace and Barney were over near the practice jumps with Judy munching some grass.

"Well come on, get on with it," Eric grumbled under his breath at one of the officials.

There were only half a dozen or so riders left. Camilla had gone home in a huff. Mrs Brayfield was standing near the table of prizes, fluttering and twittering away to the photographer. I couldn't take my eyes off the lovely silver horseshoe that was the winning trophy.

Zoe had got third place! She gaped in shock as her name was called out and I literally had to push her in the back. She received a beautiful yellow rosette and a brown envelope with some prize money and scuttled back to our group suddenly all shy.

I crossed my fingers behind my back. I couldn't believe how much I wanted to win.

"And first place goes to . . ."

A tall lad with ginger hair automatically barged forward and then stopped, unsure.

"Alexandra Johnson!"

"Ya-hoo!" Eric let out a whoop of joy that would have put Daisy to shame. Ash and Zoe were clapping like mad. Barney had done the impossible. We both had.

"Congratulations," said the local dignitary. I picked up the silver horseshoe as if it were the crown jewels, and my rosette and prize money and a lovely navy rug. We had won the Pony Club One-Day Event. It was the first rung on the ladder to the top.

"And don't think you can take it easy." Eric wagged his finger. "This is just the beginning."

Lazily with the first ebb of tiredness washing over me, I led Barney up the horsebox ramp and tied him next to Lace. Ash adjusted his new rug which looked fantastic and gave him a warm pat on the neck.

"And as for you, Miss Johnson." He suddenly took me in his arms and gave me a gentle kiss.

"Ouch," I yelped as he brushed my sore lips.

"Sorry." And then he kissed me again and it was wonderful.

"Another toast." Eric raised his glass as we sat in the living quarters drinking champagne and munching hot doughnuts from the food stand outside. He was plotting and planning as if we were already in the Junior Championships.

"To Eric." Zoe raised her glass. "The best trainer in the country."

"Hear, hear." Ash joined in.

Judy clambered in with more doughnuts and we gave her a fresh glass.

"To Barney," I spluttered, overdosing on happiness.

Eric was right. This was just the beginning. We were now serious competitors with a whole future ahead of us. We were *eventers* and what more could we possibly ask for?

GLOSSARY

anti-cast roller   A stable **roller** which prevents the horse from becoming **cast** in the stable or box.

Badminton   One of the world's greatest three-day events, staged each year at Badminton House, Gloucestershire.

to bank   When a horse lands on the middle part of an obstacle (e.g. a **table**), it is said to have banked it.

bit   The part of the bridle which fits in the mouth of the horse, and to which the reins are attached.

bridle   The leather **tack** attached to the horse's head which helps the rider to control the horse.

cast   When a horse is lying down against a wall in a stable or box and is unable to get up, it is said to be cast.

chef d'équipe   The person who manages and sometimes captains a team at events.

colic   A sickness of the digestive system. Very dangerous for horses because they cannot be sick.

collected canter A slow pace with good energy.

crop A whip.

cross-country A gallop over rough ground, jumping solid natural fences. One of the three eventing disciplines. (The others are **dressage** and **showjumping**.)

dressage A discipline in which rider and horse perform a series of movements to show how balanced, controlled, etc. they are.

dun Horse colour, generally yellow dun. (Also blue dun.)

feed room Store room for horse food.

girth The band which goes under the stomach of a horse to hold the **saddle** in place.

Grackle A type of noseband which stops the horse opening its mouth wide or crossing its jaw. Barney is wearing one on the cover of *Will to Win*.

hand A hand is 10 cm (4 in) – approximately the width of a man's hand. A horse's height is given in hands.

hard mouth A horse is said to have a hard mouth if it does not respond to the rider's commands through the **reins** and **bit**. It is caused by over-use of the reins and bit: the horse has got used to the pressure and thus ignores it.

head collar A headpiece without a **bit**, used for leading and tying-up.

horsebox A vehicle designed specifically for the transport of horses.

horse trailer A trailer holding one to three horses, designed to be towed by a separate vehicle.

jockey skull A type of riding hat, covered in brightly coloured silks or nylon.

jodhpurs Type of trousers/leggings worn when riding.

lead rope Used for leading a horse. (Also known as a "shank".)

livery Stables where horses are kept at the owners' expense.

manege Enclosure for schooling a horse.

manger Container holding food, often fixed to a stable wall.

one-day event Equestrian competition completed over one day, featuring **dressage, showjumping** and **cross-country**.

Palomino A horse with a gold-coloured body and white mane or tail.

Pelham bit A bit with a curb chain and two **reins**, for use on horses that are hard to stop.

Pony Club International youth organization, founded to encourage young people to ride.

reins Straps used by the rider to make contact with a horse's mouth and control it.

roller Leather or webbing used to keep a rug or blanket in place. Like a belt or girth which goes over the withers and under the stomach.

saddle Item of tack which the rider sits on. Gives security and comfort and assists in controlling the horse.

showjumping A course of coloured jumps that can be knocked down. Shows how careful and controlled horse and rider are.

snaffle bit The simplest type of bit.

square halt Position where the horse stands still with each leg level, forming a rectangle.

steeplechasing A horse race with a set number of obstacles including a water jump. Originally a cross-country race from steeple to steeple.

stirrups Shaped metal pieces which hang from the saddle by leather straps and into which riders place their feet.

surcingle A belt or strap used to keep a day or night rug in position. Similar to a **roller**, but without padding.

table   A type of jump built literally like a table, with a flat top surface.

tack   Horse-related items.

tack room   Where **tack** is stored.

take-off   The point when a horse lifts its forelegs and springs up to jump.

three-day event   A combined training competition, held over three consecutive days. Includes **dressage, cross-country** and **showjumping.** Sometimes includes roads and tracks.

tiger trap   A solid fence meeting in a point with a large ditch underneath. Large ones are called elephant traps.

Weymouth bit   Like a **Pelham bit,** but more severe.

Samantha Alexander

RIDERS 2

Team Spirit

"It's crazy." I stared down at the list of team members for the Pony Club One-Day Event. "It's got to be a mistake!"

"It's true." Zoe came off the phone. "Apparently it's a lesson in public relations. We've all got to learn to get on, team spirit and all that."

Alex Johnson and her arch-rival Camilla Davies have been put on the same team for the Pony Club One-Day Event. Will they be able to forget the past and form a winning team?